Edgar Allan Poe (1809–49) received a good education, first in England, then in a private school in Richmond, and later spent a year at the University of Virginia before he ran away to enlist in the army. Between 1827 and 1831, he published three volumes of poetry: *Tamerlane* (1827), *Al Aaraaf* (1829), and *Poems* (1831). From 1831 to 1835, he lived in Baltimore, where he began a lifelong struggle with poverty, disappointments in love, and addiction to alcohol. This last defect made it impossible for him to retain the editorial positions he later secured on magazines in Richmond, Philadelphia, and New York, despite the fact that the tales and book reviews he contributed greatly increased circulation. In May 1836, he married Virginia Clemm, a child of thirteen and the daughter of a paternal aunt. In April 1844, he moved his family to New York, and in January of the following year, his literary fortunes turned when his poem "The Raven" appeared in the *New York Evening News*. Overnight, he became the most talked-about man of letters in America. Early in 1847 his wife died, and the year 1848 saw the end of two unhappy love affairs.

Jay Parini, a poet and novelist, is Axinn Professor of English at Middlebury College. His books include the poetry collection *Anthracite Country*; the novel *The Last Station*; and biographies of John Steinbeck, William Faulkner, and Robert Frost, the last of which won the *Chicago Tribune*–Heartland Award for the best work of nonfiction of 2000. Among the many books he has edited are *The Columbia History of American Poetry* and *The Oxford Encyclopedia of American Literature*.

April Bernard's books of poems are *Blackbird Bye Bye*, which won the Walt Whitman Prize from the Academy of American Poets; *Psalms*; *Swan Electric*; and the forthcoming *Romanticism*. She has also published a novel, *Pirate Jenny*. A former magazine editor for many years, she is now a professor of literature at Bennington College and is also on the faculty of the Bennington MFA writing seminars.

The
Complete Poetry of
EDGAR ALLAN POE

WITH AN INTRODUCTION BY
Jay Parini

AND A NEW AFTERWORD BY
April Bernard

SIGNET CLASSICS

SIGNET CLASSICS
Published by New American Library, a division of
Penguin Group (USA) Inc., 375 Hudson Street,
New York, New York 10014, USA
Penguin Group (Canada), 90 Eglinton Avenue East, Suite 700, Toronto,
Ontario M4P 2Y3, Canada (a division of Pearson Penguin Canada Inc.)
Penguin Books Ltd., 80 Strand, London WC2R 0RL, England
Penguin Ireland, 25 St. Stephen's Green, Dublin 2,
Ireland (a division of Penguin Books Ltd.)
Penguin Group (Australia), 250 Camberwell Road, Camberwell, Victoria 3124,
Australia (a division of Pearson Australia Group Pty. Ltd.)
Penguin Books India Pvt. Ltd., 11 Community Centre, Panchsheel Park,
New Delhi - 110 017, India
Penguin Group (NZ), 67 Apollo Drive, Rosedale, North Shore 0632,
New Zealand (a division of Pearson New Zealand Ltd.)
Penguin Books (South Africa) (Pty.) Ltd., 24 Sturdee Avenue,
Rosebank, Johannesburg 2196, South Africa

Penguin Books Ltd., Registered Offices:
80 Strand, London WC2R 0RL, England

Published by Signet Classics, an imprint of New American Library,
a division of Penguin Group (USA) Inc.

First Signet Classics Printing, November 1996
First Signet Classics Printing (Bernard Afterword), October 2008
30

Introduction copyright © Jay Parini, 1996
Afterword copyright © April Bernard, 2008
All rights reserved

 REGISTERED TRADEMARK—MARCA REGISTRADA

Printed in the United States of America

CONTENTS

Contents

INTRODUCTION

I.

When Edgar Allan Poe died in 1849, only forty but ravaged in body and spirit by alcohol, his standing in the world of literature was by no means high. Indeed, it would take a major effort on the part of his admirers to revive his damaged reputation in his own country. To this day, critics argue about his literary merit, although his work has earned a solid place in the hearts of readers throughout the world.

In a sense, Poe has suffered from the vast success of a few poems. I can still remember standing before my eighth grade class, over thirty years ago, reciting the whole of "The Raven." That poem and "The Bells" were for much of the past century a staple of school curricula. Their mesmerizing rhythms have haunted generations, and may have kept them from noticing many of Poe's finer, more original works, such as "To Helen" or "The City in the Sea."

Of course Poe the poet stands in fierce contention with Poe the storyteller. Historians of literature often credit him with the invention of the modern short story, and no collection of great American fiction is complete without "The Fall of the House of Usher," "The Cask of Amontillado," and "The Pit and the Pendulum." In these genuinely frightening tales, Poe's feverish imagination is vividly on display, and his literary reputation spread rapidly throughout Europe in his own lifetime.

As a critic, Poe also achieved considerable fame. Working for the *Southern Literary Messenger,* one of several journals that he edited in his brief lifetime, Poe wrote groundbreaking essays on poetry and fiction as well as scathing reviews of contemporary writers. His most important aesthetic statement was contained in "The Poetic Principle," where he famously argued for the importance of lyric over narrative poetry, illustrating his discussion with quotations from Tennyson, Byron, Shelley, and Longfellow. Most tellingly, he held that long poems could not be good poems, at least not all the way through. "A long poem does not exist," he wrote, contentiously. "I maintain that the phrase 'a long poem' is simply a flat contradiction in terms." Here, as elsewhere, he lobbied for unity as the defining feature of major literary works, calling it "the vital requisite of all works of Art."

Poe's reputation as a writer has certainly suffered from the melodramatic quality of his life, which has made him a prime target for biographers. Born in Boston in 1809, where his parents were acting in a traveling repertory company, he was soon set adrift. His father abandoned his mother before his first birthday, and his mother died when he was three. Fortunately, a prosperous merchant, John Allan, adopted him because his wife had been a friend of the deceased Mrs. Poe, although Poe later came to detest his stepfather as much as he adored his stepmother.

The Allans took young Edgar to England in 1815, and he was put into a strict English boarding school— a setting that Poe later used for "William Wilson," his story about a double identity that Robert Louis Stevenson apparently used as a source for *Dr. Jekyll and Mr. Hyde.* (Stevenson also used Poe's story "The Gold Bug" as a model for *Treasure Island.*)

Back in Baltimore in his early teens, Poe developed a crush on Mrs. Jane Stannard, the young mother of a schoolmate, and her death a year after they met affected him deeply. Young Poe brooded incessantly on Mrs. Stannard, and these thoughts seemed to have morbidly shaped his imagination. In his poems he would often dwell on the early deaths of beautiful women and would specialize in melancholic laments for their passing.

In 1826 Poe entered the University of Virginia, but wild drinking and gambling led to his early withdrawal and added to the tensions that already existed between him and his stepfather. In 1827 he worked intermittently at odd jobs and managed to get a small Boston firm to print his first book of poetry: *Tamerlane and Other Poems.* The book made no impression on the literary world, and Poe resorted to joining the army. After rising to the rank of sergeant-major, he was honorably discharged in 1829, the same year that he published a second slim volume: *Al Aaraaf, Tamerlane, and Minor Poems.* Once again, he escaped public notice as a poet.

In what must count as one of the more peculiar turns in his life, he was appointed as a cadet at West Point in 1830. There he found himself drowning in expenses that his obviously skeptical stepfather refused to pay. "The army does not suit a poor man," he noted wryly in a letter. A year later he was court-martialed and expelled for unbecoming behavior. But he had by this time made such an impression on his fellow cadets by writing witty satirical poems about the Academy that they took up a collection to finance the publication of his third book of poems, published as *The Poems of*

Edgar A. Poe in New York in 1831. (When the cadets got their copies, they were furious because it did not contain the poems they had remembered.) Not until 1845 would he publish another volume, *The Raven and Other Poems*—the book that finally made his name as a poet.

On leaving West Point, Poe turned to prose, hoping to make a living by his pen. Book reviews, humorous anecdotes, fantasy, travel essays, and short stories poured forth, though he seemed always to be short of cash. To survive, he went to live with his favorite aunt, Mrs. Maria Clemm, and her nine-year-old daughter, Virginia, with whom he fell in love. They were married five years later—shortly before her fourteenth birthday.

Poe's unusual marriage to his cousin and his adoration of her mother are enough to drive any Freudian critic mad with speculation. In fact, biographers have little to go on here, apart from a few letters by Poe and the testimony of his friends. By every account, the young writer was devoted to his wife and aunt, and they were similarly fond of him. Virginia's tragic death a decade later was a dreadful, insurmountable obstacle in Poe's emotional life. When the French poet Charles Baudelaire published a translation of the American poet's work some years later, he dedicated the volume to Mrs. Clemm, "the woman who was always so gentle and kind to him—as you bound his wounds with your love, so he will preserve your name with his glory."

It is clear that Virginia's death in January 1847 had dire consequences on the emotional life of Edgar Poe, who died less than three years later. The years after Virginia were chaotic for him: he drank heavily, tried vainly to woo various matrons of society, and wrote little. In the summer of 1849 he made a sentimental journey to Richmond, where he had lived for many years with Virginia, and by chance encountered Sarah

Royster, a woman he had once loved many years before. After a short time, he proposed marriage and she accepted, but soon his drinking got the better of him. He was found wandering the backstreets of Baltimore in late September 1849, and he died on October 7 in the Washington College Hospital.

At the time of his death, William Cullen Bryant, Ralph Waldo Emerson, and James Russell Lowell were among the most revered American poets, and they largely refused to acknowledge Poe as a real poet. Emerson called him "the jingle man," refusing him a place in his prestigious anthology, *The American Parnassus* (1847). Lowell, at least, saw fit to mention Poe in *A Fable for Critics,* although he wrote about him somewhat derisively:

> Here comes Poe with his Raven, like Barnaby
>   Rudge—
> Three-fifths of him genius and two-fifths sheer fudge;
> Who talks like a book of iambs and pentameters
> In a way to make all men of common sense d——m
>   meters;
> Who has written some things far the best of his kind,
> But somehow the heart seems squeezed out by the
>   mind.

Even Walt Whitman, the greatest American poet of the century, dismissed him, claiming Poe ought to be regarded as "among the electric lights of literature, brilliant and dazzling, with no heat."

It was left mostly to French readers and critics to elevate Poe to the literary pantheon: Baudelaire adored and translated him, Stephane Mallarmé called him "my great master," and Paul Valéry considered him "profound and so insidiously learned." André Gide described Poe as "the only impeccable master." Eventually—some fifteen years after his death—Poe was recognized in his own country by a memorial volume edited by Sara Sigourney Rice. Bryant, John Greenleaf Whittier, Longfellow, and Oliver Wendell Holmes joined Tennyson and other Europeans to proclaim Poe's originality and genius as a poet and storyteller. Lord Tennyson struck the most vivid note when he called Poe "the most original genius that America has produced," one "not unworthy to stand beside Catullus, the most melodious of the Latins, and Heine, the most tuneful of the Germans."

II.

"Tamerlane" was Poe's first important poem, and it remains a fascinating work. The historical figure on whom the poem is based was born in Samarkand, in central Asia, in the fourteenth century. This ruthless conqueror ruled an empire extending from the Black Sea to central China, but relatively little is actually known about the historical Tamerlane. Certainly Poe knew next to nothing about him, as he admitted in his preface to that volume, and so the Tamerlane of his poem is a glorious invention. Indeed, Poe begged the reader's pardon for making his hero "speak in the same language as a Boston gentleman of the nineteenth century."

The poem, which shows the direct influence of Lord Byron, is typically Romantic in style, echoing popular themes of the period: the thirst for power, blighted love, and fate. In Poe's hand the poem becomes an allegory of the poet's own ambition and an elegy for lost love. In a telling moment, the aging conqueror admits to a Christian friar that his worldly quest for power had actually thwarted his desire to attain human love:

How was it that Ambition crept,
   Unseen, amid the revels there,
Till growing bold, he laughed and leapt
   In the tangles of Love's very hair?

"Tamerlane" was reproduced in Poe's second volume, two years later, along with another long poem, "Al Aaraaf." The title refers to a state of limbo described in the Koran, which Poe identifies here with a mysterious star discovered in 1572 by the Danish astronomer Tycho Brahe. Running to 264 lines, the poem is rambling and diffuse, echoing Shelley's *Prometheus Unbound* (1820) in many places. It is best read as a sequence of disconnected lyric moments, as in the following hymn to Ligeia, the goddess of harmony, where Poe's mastery of the two-beat line is gorgeously in evidence:

Ligeia! Ligeia!
   My beautiful one!
Whose harshest idea
   Will to melody run.
O! is it thy will
   On the breezes to toss?
Or, capriciously still
   Like the lone Albatross,
Incumbent on night
   (As she is on the air)
To keep watch with delight
   On the harmony there?

The poem celebrates a place out of time where absolute beauty may be experienced directly instead of through earthly things, which are inevitably disappointing. Poe sings this perfection in some lovely lines:

Now happiest, loveliest in yon lovely Earth,
Whence sprang the "Idea of Beauty" into birth
(Falling in wreaths thro' many a startled star,
Like woman's hair 'mid pearls, until, afar,
It lit on hills Achaian, and there dwelt),
She look'd into Infinity—and knelt.

The "She" mentioned above is one of the author's mysterious intergalactic women, an astral goddess of perfect beauty; this figure will reappear, in earthly embodiments, in Poe's later verse.

The finest poem in Poe's second volume was surely his "Sonnet—To Science," which in true Romantic fashion argues against rationalism of the kind that destroys the imagination:

Why preyest thou thus upon the poet's heart,
    Vulture, whose wings are dull realities?
How should he love thee? or how deem thee wise,
    Who wouldst not leave him in his wandering
To seek for treasure in the jewelled skies,
    Albeit he soared with an undaunted wing?
Hast thou not dragged Diana from her car?
    And driven the Hamadryad from the wood
To seek a shelter in some happier star?
    Hast thou not torn the Naiad from her flood,
The Elfin from the green grass, and from me
The summer dream beneath the tamarind tree?

The poem, which has its obvious model in William Blake's "Mock on, Mock on, Voltaire, Rousseau" (1803), is conventional enough in subject, but the sound is pure Poe, as in the mellifluous wonder of that last line, where the expected final iambic foot is replaced by an anapest. (That is, Poe adds an extra unstressed syllable before the last word, giving it a peculiar resonance and sway.)

Among the other treasures of Poe's early verse are "Israfel," "The Sleeper," "The Valley of Unrest," the first of two poems called "To Helen," and "The City in the Sea." The last (one of my favorite poems by Poe) was inspired by the *History of the Jewish War* by Flavius Josephus (written in the first century A.D.). Poe evokes a city much like the corrupt biblical city of Gomorrah, "a strange city lying alone / Far down within the dim West." The poet's vision is characteristically frenzied:

> No rays from the holy heaven come down
> On the long night-time of that town;
> But light from out the lurid sea
> Streams up the turrets silently—

The city emerges in a kind of tragic grandeur as Poe imagines a place where numerous artists once lived and worked. He describes "the Babylon-like walls" of the city "Whose wreathèd friezes intertwine / The viol, the violet, and the vine." That last line, as the English poet Swinburne noted many years later, is a small miracle of euphony.

This poem might also be read as an allegory of ambition here: the poet becomes the city, sunk beneath the lurid sea, a place where a chance of revival exists. "But lo, a stir is in the air!" the poet cries in the last stanza. Life seems to prosper in a strange way beneath this symbolic sea, and "The waves have now a redder glow," which suggests a process of recovery, even regeneration. The poem is hardly a condemnation of the excesses of Gomorrah, as one might expect from a poem written in the mid–nineteenth century. Indeed,

Poe seems to celebrate the decadence of the city and to identify with it.

"The Sleeper" belongs with "The Valley of Unrest" and "The City in the Sea" as a poem in which doom is evoked and cultivated. It portrays that mysterious state existing somewhere between life and death—a topic Poe would return to often in later poems. The speaker in "The Sleeper" has lost his beloved, and over her grave he prays these chilling, rather morbid, lines:

> My love, she sleeps! Oh, may her sleep,
> As it is lasting, so be deep!
> Soft may the worms about her creep!

The first of Poe's two poems called "To Helen" is utterly different. It opens:

> Helen, thy beauty is to me
>   Like those Nicèan barks of yore,
> That gently, o'er a perfumed sea,
>   The weary, way-worn wanderer bore
>   To his own native shore.

> On desperate seas long wont to roam,
>   Thy hyacinth hair, thy classic face,
> Thy Naiad airs have brought me home
>   To the glory that was Greece
> And the grandeur that was Rome.

The last two lines quoted above are, of course, among the most famous that Poe ever wrote. The poem itself represents a masterpiece in the elegiac love lyric mode, and it was inspired by the poet's affection for Jane Stannard, though he changed the unpoetical "Jane" to the more melodic and mythically resonant "Helen"—a name that would mutate in later poems to "Eleanora" and "Lenore."

Poe never actually ceased to write poetry during any period, but he did seem to focus on fiction and criticism in the late 1830s and early 1840s. The struggle to support himself and Virginia was consuming, and it was much easier to make a living by writing prose than poetry. He did, however, find time to compose some of his best poems, including "The Haunted Palace," "Dream-Land," and "The Raven" during these years.

"The Haunted Palace" made its first appearance in 1839, in Poe's story "The Fall of the House of Usher." It embodies the themes of that bizarre tale in compressed form, alluding to "evil things, in robes of sorrow." A. E. Housman, the English poet, remarked that this poem might be considered "one of Poe's best poems so long as we are content to swim in the sensations it evokes and only vaguely to apprehend the allegory." Houseman refers to the fact that, in the poem, the fair palace door is meant to be Roderick Usher's mouth, the pearl and ruby his teeth and lips, and the yellow banners his hair. The "ramparts plumed and pallid" are presumably Usher's forehead. (One sees what Housman meant.)

"Dream-Land," written in 1844, explores that region of irrationality and darkness that became one of Poe's favorite places of visitation. Specifically, he summons a land "From a wild weird clime that lieth, sublime, / Out of SPACE—out of TIME." The lyricism found in this poem is apparent as Poe evokes "Bottomless vales and boundless floods, / And chasms, and caves, and Titan woods." As is often the case in the work of this poet, the narrator wants desperately to escape from the real world into a world of fantasy, a dreamworld where pain is eased and one has merely to pay the price of extreme melancholy.

"The Raven" was published in 1845; it was a poem so original and memorable that Poe woke up soon after its appearance and found himself famous. It was dedicated to the English poet Elizabeth Barrett, whom Poe deeply admired; indeed, he lifted the incantatory rhythms of his poem from Barrett's own "Lady Geraldine's Courtship." (Compare Barrett's "With a murmurous stir uncertain, in the air a purple curtain" to Poe's "And the silken, sad, uncertain rustling of each purple curtain.")

When Barrett received her copy from the American author, she wrote back: "Your 'Raven' has produced a sensation, a 'fit horror,' here in England." Indeed, English and American readers alike were taken by the addictive music of the poem, and its haunting refrain of "Nevermore." Poe's symbolic bird seemed to dwell in the same heady air as Coleridge's albatross, Shelley's skylark, and Keats' nightingale; it also had much in common with a fierce raven in Charles Dickens' popular novel *Barnaby Rudge* (1841).

Poe himself characterized the poem's action in an essay written a year after the poem was published:

> A raven, having learned by rote the single word "Nevermore" and having escaped from the custody of its owner, is driven at midnight, through the violence of a storm, to seek admission at a window from which a light still gleams—the chamber-window of a student, occupied half in poring over a volume, half in dreaming of a beloved mistress deceased.

Thomas Campion, the English poet (a contemporary of Shakespeare), defined poetry as "a system of linked sounds," and that definition could hardly be more appropriate for "The Raven." Its internal rhymes, however overstated, form an intricately satisfying pattern; the reader is drawn into its spiral, and is not released until the end. The poem describes the obsessive mental state of a man who has lost his "maiden whom the angels name Lenore." The storm raging outside his window is clearly a symbolic storm, a storm of the soul. The "pallid bust of Pallas" (the goddess Athena) that plays uneasy host to the maniacal raven represents wisdom. The raven stands for the intuitive powers of memory, fate, and the dark side of the human mind, each of which preys on hope. The suffering narrator's frantic questions are all answered negatively, and he is forced to confront the brutal truth that he will not be reunited after death with Lenore, his beloved.

"The Raven" was reprinted again and again in Poe's lifetime, and has remained a favorite of readers. Oddly enough, the poem seems to have exhausted its creator; from 1845 until his death four years later, Poe wrote only a handful of poems, although most of them are excellent, including "Ulalume," an elegy for Virginia that has a poignancy and melancholy all its own. The name itself, representing the lost love of the poem's soulful narrator, was coined by Poe, although it seems to allude to the Latin word *ulalure*—to wail. One also hears an echo of *lumen,* meaning light. The poem is set in a misty atmosphere reminiscent of "the region of Weir," a reference to Robert Walter Weir, a painter of the Hudson River school.

Many of Poe's last poems were addressed to the women he had either flirted with or attempted to marry after Virginia's death. The best of them is the second "To Helen," written to honor a poet called Helen Whitman, to whom Poe grew attached after visiting her in Rhode Island in 1845. It opens with a remarkably casual few lines that are unusual in Poe in being so conversational: "I saw thee once—once only—years ago: / I must not say *how* many—but *not* many." The poem is a model of linguistic control and sensual music.

One of Poe's most widely anthologized poems is "The Bells," an onomatopoeic tour de force written in four stanzas that describe the good and bad resonances of bells of various kinds: sleigh bells, wedding bells, alarm bells, and church bells. It is a silly, late poem that Poe obviously wrote for the sheer joy of the sounds he discovered he could make in verse. While the poem is devoid of deeper levels of meaning, it remains entertaining to read and, especially, to recite aloud.

In May 1849 Poe finished his last, and one of his finest, poems, "Annabel Lee." It is an intensely autobiographical poem in which the narrator mourns the death of a beautiful young woman, his child bride. Poe's readers will have encountered this theme in many of his previous poems, including "Lenore," "The Sleeper," "To One in Paradise," "The Raven," and "Ulalume." In "Annabel Lee," however, a promise of reunion with the deceased lover is finally held out:

> But our love it was stronger by far than the love
> Of those who were older than we—
> Of many far wiser than we—
> And neither the angels in Heaven above,
> Nor the demons down under the sea,
> Can ever dissever my soul from the soul
> Of the beautiful ANNABEL LEE.

The beauty of this language, where rhythm and meaning are so perfectly attuned, has been justly praised by writers from Tennyson to Vladimir Nabokov. The poem was written to the one and only Virginia, Poe's own child bride. It was his dream of dreams, in which he recounts the joys of a lost love, a time when they were children in their "kingdom by the sea." He summons in the poem's final stanza a vision of eternal love and reunion with the woman he called "my darling, my darling, my life and my bride."

For Edgar Allan Poe, the art of poetry was ultimately about the contemplation of ideal beauty. Though obsessed with death, and with states of unreality and nightmare, he looked for moments of transcendence, believing that visionary insights were attainable only "in brief and indeterminate glimpses." In his best poems, he creates a rhythmical language in which a melodious chiming on vowel sounds and consonants works to impress his lines deep in the reader's memory, giving them the literary equivalent of eternal life. As T. S. Eliot once said, "Only after you find that a poem by Poe goes on throbbing in your head," he wrote, "do you begin to suspect that perhaps you will never forget it."

—Jay Parini

Tamerlane

Kind solace in a dying hour!
  Such, father, is not (now) my theme—
I will not madly deem that power
    Of Earth may shrive me of the sin
    Unearthly pride hath revell'd in—
  I have no time to dote or dream:
You call it hope—that fire of fire!
It is but agony of desire:
If I *can* hope—oh, God! I can—
  Its fount is holier—more divine—
I would not call thee fool, old man,
  But such is not a gift of thine.

Know thou the secret of a spirit
  Bow'd from its wild pride into shame.
O yearning heart! I did inherit
  Thy withering portion with the fame,
The searing glory which hath shone
Amid the jewels of my throne,
Halo of Hell! and with a pain
Not Hell shall make me fear again—
O craving heart, for the lost flowers
And sunshine of my summer hours!
The undying voice of that dead time,
With its interminable chime,
Rings, in the spirit of a spell,
Upon thy emptiness—a knell.

I have not always been as now:
The fever'd diadem on my brow
  I claim'd and won usurpingly—
Hath not the same fierce heirdom given
  Rome to the Caesar—this to me?

The heritage of a kingly mind,
And a proud spirit which hath striven
    Triumphantly with human kind.

On mountain soil I first drew life:
    The mists of the Taglay have shed
    Nightly their dews upon my head,
And, I believe, the winged strife
And tumult of the headlong air
Have nestled in my very hair.

So late from Heaven—that dew—it fell
    ('Mid dreams of an unholy night)
Upon me with the touch of Hell,
    While the red flashing of the light
From clouds that hung, like banners, o'er,
    Appeared to my half-closing eye
    The pageantry of monarchy,
And the deep trumpet-thunder's roar
    Came hurriedly upon me, telling
        Of human battle, where my voice,
    My own voice, silly child!—was swelling
        (O! how my spirit would rejoice,
And leap within me at the cry)
The battle-cry of Victory!

The rain came down upon my head
    Unshelter'd—and the heavy wind
    Rendered me mad and deaf and blind.
It was but man, I thought, who shed
    Laurels upon me: and the rush—
    The torrent of the chilly air
Gurgled within my ear the crush
    Of empires—with the captive's prayer—
The hum of suitors—and the tone
Of flattery 'round a sovereign's throne.

My passions, from that hapless hour,
   Usurp'd a tyranny which men
Have deem'd, since I have reach'd to power,
    My innate nature—be it so:
   But, father, there liv'd one who, then,
Then—in my boyhood—when their fire
    Burn'd with a still intenser glow
(For passion must, with youth, expire)
   E'en *then* who knew this iron heart
   In woman's weakness had a part.

I have no words—alas!—to tell
The loveliness of loving well!
Nor would I now attempt to trace
The more than beauty of a face
Whose lineaments, upon my mind,
Are—shadows on th' unstable wind:
Thus I remember having dwelt
   Some page of early lore upon,
With loitering eye, till I have felt
The letters—with their meaning—melt
   To fantasies—with none.

O, she was worthy of all love!
   Love—as in infancy was mine—
'Twas such as angel minds above
   Might envy; her young heart the shrine
On which my every hope and thought
   Were incense—then a goodly gift,
    For they were childish and upright—
Pure—as her young example taught:
   Why did I leave it, and, adrift,
    Trust to the fire within, for light?

We grew in age—and love—together—
   Roaming the forest, and the wild;

My breast her shield in wintry weather—
  And, when the friendly sunshine smil'd,
And she would mark the opening skies,
I saw no Heaven—but in her eyes.

Young Love's first lesson is—the heart:
  For 'mid that sunshine, and those smiles,
When, from our little cares apart,
  And laughing at her girlish wiles,
I'd throw me on her throbbing breast,
  And pour my spirit out in tears—
There was no need to speak the rest—
  No need to quiet any fears
Of her—who ask'd no reason why,
But turn'd on me her quiet eye!

Yet *more* than worthy of the love
My spirit struggled with, and strove,
When, on the mountain peak, alone,
Ambition lent it a new tone—
I had no being—but in thee:
  The world, and all it did contain
In the earth—the air—the sea—
  Its joy—its little lot of pain
That was new pleasure—the ideal,
  Dim, vanities of dreams by night—
And dimmer nothings which were real—
  (Shadows—and a more shadowy light!)
Parted upon their misty wings,
      And, so, confusedly, became
      Thine image and—a name— name!
Two separate—yet most intimate things.

I was ambitious—have you known
      The passion, father? You have not:
A cottager, I mark'd a throne

Of half the world as all my own,
    And murmur'd at such lowly lot—
But, just like any other dream,
    Upon the vapor of the dew
My own had past, did not the beam
    Of beauty which did while it thro'
The minute—the hour—the day—oppress
My mind with double loveliness.

We walk'd together on the crown
Of a high mountain which look'd down
Afar from its proud natural towers
    Of rock and forest, on the hills—
The dwindled hills! begirt with bowers
    And shouting with a thousand rills.

I spoke to her of power and pride,
    But mystically—in such guise
That she might deem it nought beside
    The moment's converse; in her eyes
I read, perhaps too carelessly,
    A mingled feeling with my own—
The flush on her bright cheek, to me
    Seem'd to become a queenly throne
Too well that I should let it be
    Light in the wilderness alone.

I wrapp'd myself in grandeur then
    And donn'd a visionary crown—
        Yet it was not that Fantasy
        Had thrown her mantle over me—
But that, among the rabble—men,
    Lion ambition is chain'd down—
And crouches to a keeper's hand—
Not so in deserts where the grand—

The wild—the terrible conspire
With their own breath to fan his fire.

Look 'round thee now on Samarcand!—
    Is she not queen of Earth? her pride
Above all cities? in her hand
    Their destinies? in all beside
Of glory which the world hath known
Stands she not nobly and alone?
Falling—her veriest stepping-stone
Shall form the pedestal of a throne—
And who her sovereign? Timour—he
    Whom the astonished people saw
Striding o'er empires haughtily
    A diadem'd outlaw!

O, human love! thou spirit given,
On Earth, of all we hope in Heaven!
Which fall'st into the soul like rain
Upon the Siroc-wither'd plain,
And, failing in thy power to bless,
But leav'st the heart a wilderness!
Idea! which bindest life around
With music of so strange a sound
And beauty of so wild a birth—
Farewell! for I have won the Earth.

When Hope, the eagle that tower'd, could see
    No cliff beyond him in the sky,
His pinions were bent droopingly—
    And homeward turn'd his soften'd eye.
'Twas sunset: when the sun will part
There comes a sullenness of heart
To him who still would look upon
The glory of the summer sun.
That soul will hate the ev'ning mist

So often lovely, and will list
To the sound of the coming darkness (known
To those whose spirits harken) as one
Who, in a dream of night, *would* fly
But *cannot* from a danger nigh.

What tho' the moon—the white moon—
Shed all the splendor of her noon,
Her smile is chilly—and *her* beam,
In that time of dreariness, will seem
(So like you gather in your breath)
A portrait taken after death.
And boyhood is a summer sun
Whose waning is the dreariest one.
For all we live to know is known,
And all we seek to keep hath flown.
Let life, then, as the day-flower, fall
With the noon-day beauty—which is all.

I reach'd my home—my home no more—
    For all had flown who made it so.
I pass'd from out its mossy door,
    And, tho' my tread was soft and low,
A voice came from the threshold stone
Of one whom I had earlier known—
    O, I defy thee, Hell, to show
    On beds of fire that burn below,
    An humbler heart—a deeper wo.

Father, I firmly do believe—
    I *know*—for Death who comes for me
    From regions of the blest afar,
Where there is nothing to deceive,
    Hath left his iron gate ajar,
    And rays of truth you cannot see
    Are flashing thro' Eternity—

I do believe that Eblis hath
A snare in every human path—
Else how, when in the holy grove
I wandered of the idol, Love,
Who daily scents his snowy wings
With incense of burnt offerings
From the most unpolluted things,
Whose pleasant bowers are yet so riven
Above with trellis'd rays from Heaven
No mote may shun—no tiniest fly—
The light'ning of his eagle eye—
How was it that Ambition crept,
   Unseen, amid the revels there,
Till growing bold, he laughed and leapt
   In the tangles of Love's very hair?

Song

I saw thee on thy bridal day—
    When a burning blush came o'er thee,
Though happiness around thee lay,
    The world all love before thee:

And in thine eye a kindling light
    (Whatever it might be)
Was all on Earth my aching sight
    Of Loveliness could see.

That blush, perhaps, was maiden shame—
    As such it well may pass—
Though its glow hath raised a fiercer flame
    In the breast of him, alas!

Who saw thee on that bridal day,
    When that deep blush *would* come o'er thee,
Though happiness around thee lay,
    The world all love before thee.

Dreams

Oh! that my young life were a lasting dream!
My spirit not awak'ning till the beam
Of an Eternity should bring the morrow.
Yes! tho' that long dream were of hopeless sorrow,
'T were better than the cold reality
Of waking life, to him whose heart must be,
And hath been still, upon the lovely earth,
A chaos of deep passion, from his birth.
But should it be—that dream eternally
Continuing—as dreams have been to me
In my young boyhood—should it thus be giv'n,
'T were folly still to hope for higher Heav'n.
For I have revell'd, when the sun was bright
I' the summer sky, in dreams of living light
And loveliness,—have left my very heart
In climes of mine imagining, apart
From mine own home, with beings that have been
Of mine own thought—what more could I have
    seen?
'T was once—and only once—and the wild hour
From my remembrance shall not pass—some pow'r
Or spell had bound me—'t was the chilly wind
Came o'er me in the night, and left behind
Its image on my spirit—or the moon
Shone on my slumbers in her lofty noon
Too coldly—or the stars—howe'er it was,
That dream was as that night-wind—let it pass.

I *have been* happy, tho' but in a dream.
I have been happy—and I love the theme:
Dreams! in their vivid coloring of life,
As in that fleeting, shadowy, misty strife
Of semblance with reality which brings
To the delirious eye, more lovely things
Of Paradise and Love—and all our own!
Than young Hope in his sunniest hour hath known.

Spirits of the Dead

I

Thy soul shall find itself alone
'Mid dark thoughts of the gray tombstone—
Not one, of all the crowd, to pry
Into thine hour of secrecy.

II

Be silent in that solitude,
  Which is not loneliness—for then
The spirits of the dead who stood
  In life before thee are again
In death around thee—and their will
Shall overshadow thee: be still.

III

The night, tho' clear, shall frown—
And the stars shall look not down
From their high thrones in the heaven,
With light like Hope to mortals given—
But their red orbs, without beam,
To thy weariness shall seem
As a burning and a fever
Which would cling to thee for ever.

IV

Now are thoughts thou shalt not banish,
Now are visions ne'er to vanish;
From thy spirit shall they pass
No more—like dew-drop from the grass.

V

The breeze—the breath of God—is still—
And the mist upon the hill,
Shadowy—shadowy—yet unbroken,
Is a symbol and a token—
How it hangs upon the trees,
A mystery of mysteries!

Evening Star

'T was noontide of summer,
   And mid-time of night;
And stars, in their orbits,
   Shone pale, thro' the light
Of the brighter, cold moon,
   'Mid planets her slaves,
Herself in the Heavens,
   Her beam on the waves.
   I gaz'd a while
   On her cold smile;
Too cold—too cold for me.
   There pass'd as a shroud,
   A fleecy cloud,
And I turn'd away to thee,
   Proud Evening Star,
   In thy glory afar,
And dearer thy beam shall be;
   For joy to my heart
   Is the proud part
Thou bearest in Heav'n at night,
   And more I admire
   Thy distant fire
Than that colder, lowly light.

A Dream Within a Dream

Take this kiss upon the brow!
And, in parting from you now,
Thus much let me avow—
You are not wrong, who deem
That my days have been a dream;
Yet if Hope has flown away
In a night, or in a day,
In a vision, or in none,
Is it therefore the less *gone*?
All that we see or seem
Is but a dream within a dream.
I stand amid the roar
Of a surf-tormented shore,
And I hold within my hand
Grains of the golden sand—
How few! yet how they creep
Through my fingers to the deep,
While I weep—while I weep!
O God! can I not grasp
Them with a tighter clasp?
O God! can I not save
One from the pitiless wave?
Is *all* that we see or seem
But a dream within a dream?

Stanzas

How often we forget all time, when lone
Admiring Nature's universal throne;
Her woods—her wilds—her mountains—the intense
Reply of HERS *to* OUR *intelligence!*

I

In youth have I known one with whom the Earth,
In secret, communing held—as he with it,
In daylight, and in beauty from his birth:
Whose fervid, flick'ring torch of life was lit
From the sun and stars, whence he had drawn forth
A passionate light—such for his spirit was fit—
And yet that spirit knew not—in the hour
Of its own fervor—what had o'er it power.

II

Perhaps it may be that my mind is wrought
To a fever by the moonbeam that hangs o'er,
But I will half believe that wild light fraught
With more of sov'reignty than ancient lore
Hath ever told—or is it of a thought
The unembodied essence, and no more,
That with a quick'ning spell doth o'er us pass
As dew of the night-time, o'er the summer grass?

III

Doth o'er us pass, when, as th' expanding eye
To the lov'd object—so the tear to the lid
Will start, which lately slept in apathy?
And yet it need not be—that object—hid

From us in life—but common—which doth lie
Each hour before us—but *then* only, bid
With a strange sound, as of a harp-string broken,
T' awake us— 'T is a symbol and a token

IV

Of what in other worlds shall be—and giv'n
In beauty by our God, to those alone
Who otherwise would fall from life and Heav'n
Drawn by their heart's passion, and that tone,
That high tone of the spirit which hath striv'n,
Tho' not with Faith—with godliness—whose throne
With desp'rate energy 't hath beaten down;
Wearing its own deep feeling as a crown.

A Dream

In visions of the dark night
   I have dreamed of joy departed,
But a waking dream of life and light
   Hath left me broken-hearted.

Ah! what is not a dream by day
   To him whose eyes are cast
On things around him with a ray
   Turned back upon the past?

That holy dream—that holy dream,
   While all the world were chiding,
Hath cheered me as a lovely beam
   A lonely spirit guiding.

What though that light, thro' storm and night,
   So trembled from afar,
What could there be more purely bright
   In Truth's day-star?

"The Happiest Day, the Happiest Hour"

The happiest day—the happiest hour
   My sear'd and blighted heart hath known,
The highest hope of pride and power,
   I feel hath flown.

Of power! said I? yes! such I ween;
   But they have vanish'd long, alas!
The visions of my youth have been—
   But let them pass.

And, pride, what have I now with thee?
   Another brow may ev'n inherit
The venom thou hast pour'd on me—
   Be still, my spirit!

The happiest day—the happiest hour
   Mine eyes shall see—have ever seen,
The brightest glance of pride and power,
   I feel—have been:

But were that hope of pride and power
   Now offer'd, with the pain
Ev'n *then* I felt—that brightest hour
   I would not live again:

For on its wing was dark alloy,
   And as it flutter'd—fell
An essence—powerful to destroy
   A soul that knew it well.

The Lake: To —

In spring of youth it was my lot
To haunt of the wide world a spot
The which I could not love the less—
So lovely was the loneliness
Of a wild lake, with black rock bound,
And the tall pines that towered around.

But when the Night had thrown her pall
Upon that spot, as upon all,
And the mystic wind went by
Murmuring in melody,
Then—ah, then—I would awake
To the terror of the lone lake.

Yet that terror was not fright,
But a tremulous delight—
A feeling not the jewelled mine
Could teach or bribe me to define—
Nor Love—although the Love were thine.

Death was in that poisonous wave,
And in its gulf a fitting grave
For him who thence could solace bring
To his lone imagining,
Whose solitary soul could make
An Eden of that dim lake.

Sonnet—To Science

Science! true daughter of Old Time thou art!
   Who alterest all things with thy peering eyes.
Why preyest thou thus upon the poet's heart,
   Vulture, whose wings are dull realities?
How should he love thee? or how deem thee wise,
   Who wouldst not leave him in his wandering
To seek for treasure in the jewelled skies,
   Albeit he soared with an undaunted wing?
Hast thou not dragged Diana from her car?
   And driven the Hamadryad from the wood
To seek a shelter in some happier star?
   Hast thou not torn the Naiad from her flood,
The Elfin from the green grass, and from me
The summer dream beneath the tamarind tree?

Al Aaraaf

PART I

O! Nothing earthly save the ray
(Thrown back from flowers) of Beauty's eye,
As in those gardens where the day
Springs from the gems of Circassy—
O! nothing earthly save the thrill
Of melody in woodland rill—
Or (music of the passion-hearted)
Joy's voice so peacefully departed
That, like the murmur in the shell,
Its echo dwelleth and will dwell—
Oh, nothing of the dross of ours—
Yet all the beauty—all the flowers
That list our Love, and deck our bowers—
Adorn yon world afar, afar—
The wandering star.

'Twas a sweet time for Nesace—for there
Her world lay lolling on the golden air,
Near four bright suns—a temporary rest—
An oasis in desert of the blest.
Away—away—'mid seas of rays that roll
Empyrean splendor o'er th' unchained soul—
The soul that scarce (the billows are so dense)
Can struggle to its destin'd eminence—
To distant spheres, from time to time, she rode,
And late to ours, the favor'd one of God—
But, now, the ruler of an anchor'd realm,
She throws aside the sceptre—leaves the helm,
And, amid incense and high spiritual hymns,
Laves in quadruple light her angel limbs.

Now happiest, loveliest in yon lovely Earth,
Whence sprang the "Idea of Beauty" into birth
(Falling in wreaths thro' many a startled star,
Like woman's hair 'mid pearls, until, afar,
It lit on hills Achaian, and there dwelt),
She look'd into Infinity—and knelt.
Rich clouds, for canopies, about her curled—
Fit emblems of the model of her world—
Seen but in beauty—not impeding sight
Of other beauty glittering thro' the light—
A wreath that twined each starry form around,
And all the opal'd air in color bound.

All hurriedly she knelt upon a bed
Of flowers: of lilies such as rear'd the head
On the fair Capo Deucato, and sprang
So eagerly around about to hang
Upon the flying footsteps of—deep pride—
Of her who lov'd a mortal—and so died.
The Sephalica, budding with young bees,
Uprear'd its purple stem around her knees:
And gemmy flower, of Trebizond misnam'd—
Inmate of highest stars, where erst it sham'd
All other loveliness: its honied dew
(The fabled nectar that the heathen knew)
Deliriously sweet, was dropp'd from Heaven,
And fell on gardens of the unforgiven
In Trebizond—and on a sunny flower
So like its own above, that, to this hour,
It still remaineth, torturing the bee
With madness, and unwonted reverie:
In Heaven, and all its environs, the leaf
And blossom of the fairy plant, in grief
Disconsolate linger—grief that hangs her head,
Repenting follies that full long have fled,
Heaving her white breast to the balmy air,

Like guilty beauty, chasten'd, and more fair:
Nyctanthes too, as sacred as the light
She fears to perfume, perfuming the night:
And Clytia pondering between many a sun,
While pettish tears adown her petals run:
And that aspiring flower that sprang on Earth—
And died, ere scarce exalted into birth,
Bursting its odorous heart in spirit to wing
Its way to Heaven, from garden of a king:
And Valisnerian lotus thither flown
From struggling with the waters of the Rhone:
And thy most lovely purple perfume, Zante!
Isola d'oro!—Fior di Levante!
And the Nelumbo bud that floats for ever
With Indian Cupid down the holy river—
Fair flowers, and fairy! to whose care is given
To bear the Goddess' song, in odors, up to Heaven:

> "Spirit! that dwellest where,
>   In the deep sky,
> The terrible and fair,
>   In beauty vie!
> Beyond the line of blue—
>   The boundary of the star
> Which turneth at the view
>   Of thy barrier and thy bar—
> Of the barrier overgone
>   By the comets who were cast
> From their pride, and from their throne
>   To be drudges till the last—
> To be carriers of fire
>   (The red fire of their heart)
> With speed that may not tire
>   And with pain that shall not part—
> Who livest—*that* we know—
>   In Eternity—we feel—

But the shadow of whose brow
    What spirit shall reveal?
Tho' the beings whom thy Nesace,
    Thy messenger, hath known,
Have dream'd for thy Infinity
    A model of their own—
Thy will is done, oh, God!
    The star hath ridden high
Thro' many a tempest, but she rode
    Beneath thy burning eye;
And here, in thought, to thee—
    In thought that can alone
Ascend thy empire and so be
    A partner of thy throne—
By winged Fantasy,
    My embassy is given,
Till secrecy shall knowledge be
    In the environs of Heaven."

She ceas'd—and buried then her burning cheek
Abash'd, amid the lilies there, to seek
A shelter from the fervour of His eye;
For the stars trembled at the Deity.
She stirr'd not—breath'd not—for a voice was there
How solemnly pervading the calm air!
A sound of silence on the startled ear
Which dreamy poets name "the music of the
    sphere."
Ours is a world of words: Quiet we call
"Silence"—which is the merest word of all.
All Nature speaks, and ev'n ideal things
Flap shadowy sounds from visionary wings—
But ah! not so when, thus, in realms on high
The eternal voice of God is passing by,
And the red winds are withering in the sky!

"What tho' in worlds which sightless cycles run,
Link'd to a little system, and one sun—
Where all my love is folly, and the crowd
Still think my terrors but the thunder cloud,
The storm, the earthquake, and the ocean-wrath—
(Ah! will they cross me in my angrier path?)
What tho' in worlds which own a single sun
The sands of Time grow dimmer as they run,
Yet thine is my resplendency, so given
To bear my secrets thro' the upper Heaven.
Leave tenantless thy crystal home, and fly,
With all thy train, athwart the moony sky—
Apart—like fire-flies in Sicilian night,
And wing to other worlds another light!
Divulge the secrets of thy embassy
To the proud orbs that twinkle—and so be
To ev'ry heart a barrier and a ban
Lest the stars totter in the guilt of man!"

Up rose the maiden in the yellow night,
The single-mooned eve!—on Earth we plight
Our faith to one love—and one moon adore—
The birth-place of young Beauty had no more.
As sprang that yellow star from downy hours
Up rose the maiden from her shrine of flowers,
And bent o'er sheeny mountain and dim plain
Her way—but left not yet her Therasaean reign.

PART II

High on a mountain of enamell'd head—
Such as the drowsy shepherd on his bed
Of giant pasturage lying at his ease,
Raising his heavy eyelid, starts and sees
With many a mutter'd "hope to be forgiven,"
What time the moon is quadrated in Heaven—

Of rosy head, that towering far away
Into the sunlit ether, caught the ray
Of sunken suns at eve—at noon of night,
While the moon danc'd with the fair stranger light—
Uprear'd upon such height arose a pile
Of gorgeous columns on th' unburthen'd air,
Flashing from Parian marble that twin smile
Far down upon the wave that sparkled there,
And nursled the young mountain in its lair.
Of molten stars their pavement, such as fall
Thro' the ebon air, besilvering the pall
Of their own dissolution, while they die—
Adorning then the dwellings of the sky.
A dome, by linked light from Heaven let down,
Sat gently on these columns as a crown—
A window of one circular diamond, there,
Look'd out above into the purple air,
And rays from God shot down that meteor chain
And hallow'd all the beauty twice again,
Save when, between th' Empyrean and that ring,
Some eager spirit flapp'd his dusky wing.
But on the pillars Seraph eyes have seen
The dimness of this world: that greyish green
That Nature loves the best for Beauty's grave
Lurk'd in each cornice, round each architrave—
And every sculptur'd cherub thereabout
That from his marble dwelling peerèd out,
Seem'd earthly in the shadow of his niche—
Achaian statues in a world so rich!
Friezes from Tadmor and Persepolis—
From Balbec, and the stilly, clear abyss
Of beautiful Gomorrah! O, the wave
Is now upon thee—but too late to save!

Sound loves to revel in a summer night:
Witness the murmur of the grey twilight

That stole upon the ear, in Eyraco,
Of many a wild star-gazer long ago—
That stealeth ever on the ear of him
Who, musing, gazeth on the distance dim,
And sees the darkness coming as a cloud—
Is not its form—its voice—most palpable and loud?

But what is this?—it cometh—and it brings
A music with it—'tis the rush of wings—
A pause—and then a sweeping, falling strain,
And Nesace is in her halls again.
From the wild energy of wanton haste
   Her cheeks were flushing, and her lips apart;
And zone that clung around her gentle waist
   Had burst beneath the heaving of her heart.
Within the centre of that hall to breathe
She paus'd and panted, Zanthe! all beneath,
The fairy light that kiss'd her golden hair
And long'd to rest, yet could but sparkle there!

Young flowers were whispering in melody
To happy flowers that night—and tree to tree;
Fountains were gushing music as they fell
In many a star-lit grove, or moon-lit dell;
Yet silence came upon material things—
Fair flowers, bright waterfalls and angel wings—
And sound alone, that from the spirit sprang,
Bore burthen to the charm the maiden sang:

       " 'Neath blue-bell or streamer—
            Or tufted wild spray
       That keeps from the dreamer
            The moonbeam away—
       Bright beings! that ponder,
            With half closing eyes,

On the stars which your wonder
    Hath drawn from the skies,
Till they glance thro' the shade, and
    Come down to your brow
Like—eyes of the maiden
    Who calls on you now—
Arise! from your dreaming
    In violet bowers,
To duty beseeming
    These star-litten hours—
And shake from your tresses,
    Encumber'd with dew,
The breath of those kisses
    That cumber them too
(O, how, without you, Love!
    Could angels be blest?)—
Those kisses of true love
    That lull'd ye to rest!
Up!—shake from your wing
    Each hindering thing:
The dew of the night—
    It would weigh down your flight;
And true love caresses—
    O! leave them apart:
They are light on the tresses,
    But lead on the heart.

"Ligeia! Ligeia!
    My beautiful one!
Whose harshest idea
    Will to melody run,
O! is it thy will
    On the breezes to toss?
Or, capriciously still,
    Like the lone Albatross,

Incumbent on night
    (As she on the air)
To keep watch with delight
    On the harmony there?

"Ligeia! wherever
    Thy image may be,
No magic shall sever
    Thy music from thee.
Thou hast bound many eyes
    In a dreamy sleep—
But the strains shall arise
    Which *thy* vigilance keep:
The sound of the rain
    Which leaps down to the flower,
And dances again
    In the rhythm of the shower—
The murmur that springs
    From the growing of grass
Are the music of things—
    But are modell'd, alas!—
Away, then, my dearest,
    O! hie thee away
To springs that lie clearest
    Beneath the moon-ray—
To lone lake that smiles,
    In its dream of deep rest,
At the many star-isles
    That enjewel its breast—
Where wild flowers, creeping,
    Have mingled their shade,
On its margin is sleeping
    Full many a maid—
Some have left the cool glade, and
    Have slept with the bee—
Arouse them, my maiden,

On moorland and lea—
Go! breathe on their slumber,
    All softly in ear,
The musical number
    They slumber'd to hear—
For what can awaken
    An angel so soon,
Whose sleep hath been taken
    Beneath the cold moon,
As the spell which no slumber
    Of witchery may test,
The rhythmical number
    Which lull'd him to rest?"

Spirits in wing, and angels to the view,
A thousand seraphs burst th' Empyrean thro',
Young dreams still hovering on their drowsy flight—
Seraphs in all but "Knowledge," the keen light
That fell, refracted, thro' thy bounds, afar
O Death! from eye of God upon that star:
Sweet was that error—sweeter still that death—
Sweet was that error—ev'n with *us* the breath
Of Science dims the mirror of our joy—
To them 'twere the Simoom, and would destroy—
For what (to them) availeth it to know
That Truth is Falsehood—or that Bliss is Woe?
Sweet was their death—with them to die was rife
With the last ecstasy of satiate life—
Beyond that death no immortality—
But sleep that pondereth and is not "to be"—
And there—oh! may my weary spirit dwell—
Apart from Heaven's Eternity—and yet how far from
   Hell!

What guilty spirit, in what shrubbery dim,
Heard not the stirring summons of that hymn?

But two: they fell: for Heaven no grace imparts
To those who hear not for their beating hearts.
A maiden-angel and her seraph-lover—
O! where (and ye may seek the wide skies over)
Was Love, the blind, near sober Duty known?
Unguided Love hath fallen—'mid "tears of perfect
    moan."

He was a goodly spirit—he who fell:
A wanderer by moss-y-mantled well—
A gazer on the lights that shine above—
A dreamer in the moonbeam by his love:
What wonder? for each star is eye-like there,
And looks so sweetly down on Beauty's hair;
And they, and ev'ry mossy spring were holy
To his love-haunted heart and melancholy.
The night had found (to him a night of wo)
Upon a mountain crag, young Angelo—
Beetling it bends athwart the solemn sky,
And scowls on starry worlds that down beneath it lie.
Here sate he with his love—his dark eye bent
With eagle gaze along the firmament:
Now turn'd it upon her—but ever then
It trembled to the orb of EARTH again.

"Ianthe, dearest, see! how dim that ray!
How lovely 'tis to look so far away!
She seem'd not thus upon that autumn eve
I left her gorgeous halls—nor mourn'd to leave.
That eve—that eve—I should remember well—
The sun-ray dropp'd in Lemnos, with a spell
On th' Arabesque carving of a gilded hall
Wherein I sate, and on the draperied wall—
And on my eyelids—O the heavy light!
How drowsily it weigh'd them into night!
On flowers, before, and mist, and love they ran

With Persian Saadi in his Gulistan:
But O that light!—I slumber'd—Death, the while,
Stole o'er my senses in that lovely isle
So softly that no single silken hair
Awoke that slept—or knew that he was there.

"The last spot of Earth's orb I trod upon
Was a proud temple call'd the Parthenon.
More beauty clung around her column'd wall
Than ev'n thy glowing bosom beats withal,
And when old Time my wing did disenthral—
Thence sprang I—as the eagle from his tower,
And years I left behind me in an hour.
What time upon her airy bounds I hung,
One half the garden of her globe was flung,
Unrolling as a chart into my view—
Tenantless cities of the desert too!
Ianthe, beauty crowded on me then,
And half I wish'd to be again of men."

"My Angelo! and why of them to be?
A brighter dwelling-place is here for thee—
And greener fields than in yon world above,
And woman's loveliness—and passionate love."

"But, list, Ianthe! when the air so soft
Fail'd, as my pennon'd spirit leapt aloft,
Perhaps my brain grew dizzy—but the world
I left so late was into chaos hurl'd—
Sprang from her station, on the winds apart,
And roll'd, a flame, the fiery Heaven athwart.
Methought, my sweet one, then I ceased to soar,
And fell—not swiftly as I rose before,
But with a downward, tremulous motion thro'
Light, brazen rays, this golden star unto!
Nor long the measure of my falling hours,

For nearest of all stars was thine to ours—
Dread star! that came, amid a night of mirth,
A red Daedalion on the timid Earth."

"We came—and to thy Earth—but not to us
Be given our lady's bidding to discuss:
We came, my love; around, above, below,
Gay fire-fly of the night we come and go,
Nor ask a reason save the angel-nod
She grants to us, as granted by her God—
But, Angelo, than thine grey Time unfurl'd
Never his fairy wing o'er fairier world!
Dim was its little disk, and angel eyes
Alone could see the phantom in the skies,
When first Al Aaraaf knew her course to be
Headlong thitherward o'er the starry sea—
But when its glory swell'd upon the sky,
As glowing Beauty's bust beneath man's eye,
We paus'd before the heritage of men,
And thy star trembled—as doth Beauty then!"

Thus, in discourse, the lovers whiled away
The night that waned and waned and brought no day.
They fell: for Heaven to them no hope imparts
Who hear not for the beating of their hearts.

Romance

Romance, who loves to nod and sing,
With drowsy head and folded wing,
Among the green leaves as they shake
Far down within some shadowy lake,
To me a painted paroquet
Hath been—a most familiar bird—
Taught me my alphabet to say,
To lisp my very earliest word,
While in the wild wood I did lie,
A child—with a most knowing eye.

Of late, eternal Condor years
So shake the very Heaven on high
With tumult as they thunder by,
I have no time for idle cares
Through gazing on the unquiet sky.
And when an hour with calmer wings
Its down upon my spirit flings—
That little time with lyre and rhyme
To while away—forbidden things!
My heart would feel to be a crime
Unless it trembled with the strings.

To ——

The bowers whereat, in dreams, I see
   The wantonest singing birds,
Are lips—and all thy melody
   Of lip-begotten words.

Thine eyes, in Heaven of heart enshrined,
   Then desolately fall,
O, God! on my funereal mind
   Like starlight on a pall.

Thy heart—*thy* heart!—I wake and sigh,
   And sleep to dream till day
Of the truth that gold can never buy—
   Of the baubles that it may.

To the River —

Fair river! in thy bright, clear flow
  Of crystal, wandering water,
Thou art an emblem of the glow
    Of beauty—the unhidden heart—
    The playful maziness of art
  In old Alberto's daughter;
But when within thy wave she looks—
  Which glistens then, and trembles—
Why, then, the prettiest of brooks
  Her worshipper resembles;
For in his heart, as in thy stream,
  Her image deeply lies—
His heart which trembles at the beam
  Of her soul-searching eyes.

To ——

I heed not that my earthly lot
    Hath—little of Earth in it—
That years of love have been forgot
    In the hatred of a minute:—
I mourn not that the desolate
    Are happier, sweet, than I,
But that *you* sorrow for *my* fate
    Who am a passer by.

Fairy-Land

Dim vales—and shadowy floods—
And cloudy-looking woods,
Whose forms we can't discover
For the tears that drip all over:
Huge moons there wax and wane—
Again—again—again—
Every moment of the night—
Forever changing places—
And they put out the star-light
With the breath from their pale faces.
About twelve by the moon-dial,
One more filmy than the rest
(A kind which, upon trial,
They have found to be the best)
Comes down—still down—and down
With its centre on the crown
Of a mountain's eminence,
While its wide circumference
In easy drapery falls
Over hamlets, over halls,
Wherever they may be—
O'er the strange woods—o'er the sea—
Over spirits on the wing—
Over every drowsy thing—
And buries them up quite
In a labyrinth of light—
And then, how deep!—O, deep,
Is the passion of their sleep!
In the morning they arise,
And their moony covering
Is soaring in the skies,
With the tempests as they toss,
Like—almost any thing—

Or a yellow Albatross.
They use that moon no more
For the same end as before,
Videlicet, a tent—
Which I think extravagant:
Its atomies, however,
Into a shower dissever,
Of which those butterflies
Of Earth, who seek the skies,
And so come down again
(Never-contented things!)
Have brought a specimen
Upon their quivering wings.

Alone

From childhood's hour I have not been
As others were—I have not seen
As others saw—I could not bring
My passions from a common spring—
From the same source I have not taken
My sorrow—I could not awaken
My heart to joy at the same tone—
And all I lov'd—*I* lov'd alone.
Then—in my childhood—in the dawn
Of a most stormy life—was drawn
From ev'ry depth of good and ill
The mystery which binds me still—
From the torrent, or the fountain—
From the red cliff of the mountain—
From the sun that round me roll'd
In its autumn tint of gold—
From the lightning in the sky
As it pass'd me flying by—
From the thunder, and the storm—
And the cloud that took the form
(When the rest of Heaven was blue)
Of a demon in my view.

To Helen

Helen, thy beauty is to me
  Like those Nicèan barks of yore,
That gently, o'er a perfumed sea,
  The weary, way-worn wanderer bore
  To his own native shore.

On desperate seas long wont to roam,
  Thy hyacinth hair, thy classic face,
Thy Naiad airs have brought me home
  To the glory that was Greece,
And the grandeur that was Rome.

Lo! in yon brilliant window-niche
  How statue-like I see thee stand,
  The agate lamp within thy hand!
Ah, Psyche, from the regions which
  Are Holy-Land!

Israfel

*And the angel Israfel, whose
heart-strings are a lute, and
who has the sweetest voice
of all God's creatures.*—KORAN

In Heaven a spirit doth dwell
  "Whose heart-strings are a lute;"
None sing so wildly well
As the angel Israfel,
And the giddy stars (so legends tell),
Ceasing their hymns, attend the spell
  Of his voice, all mute.

Tottering above
  In her highest noon,
  The enamoured moon
Blushes with love,
  While, to listen, the red levin
  (With the rapid Pleiads, even,
  Which were seven,)
  Pauses in Heaven.

And they say (the starry choir
  And the other listening things)
That Israfeli's fire
Is owing to that lyre
  By which he sits and sings—
The trembling living wire
  Of those unusual strings.

But the skies that angel trod,
  Where deep thoughts are a duty—
Where Love's a grown-up God—

Where the Houri glances are
Imbued with all the beauty
  Which we worship in a star.

Therefore, thou are not wrong,
  Israfeli, who despisest
An unimpassioned song;
To thee the laurels belong,
  Best bard, because the wisest!
Merrily live, and long!

The ecstasies above
  With thy burning measures suit—
Thy grief, thy joy, thy hate, thy love,
  With the fervour of thy lute—
  Well may the stars be mute!

Yes, Heaven is thine; but this
  Is a world of sweets and sours;
  Our flowers are merely—flowers,
And the shadow of thy perfect bliss
  Is the sunshine of ours.

If I could dwell
Where Israfel
  Hath dwelt, and he where I,
He might not sing so wildly well
  A mortal melody,
While a bolder note than this might swell
  From my lyre within the sky.

The City in the Sea

Lo! Death has reared himself a throne
In a strange city lying alone
Far down within the dim West,
Where the good and the bad and the worst and the
    best
Have gone to their eternal rest.
There shrines and palaces and towers
(Time-eaten towers that tremble not!)
Resemble nothing that is ours.
Around, by lifting winds forgot,
Resignedly beneath the sky
The melancholy waters lie.

No rays from the holy heaven come down
On the long night-time of that town;
But light from out the lurid sea
Streams up the turrets silently—
Gleams up the pinnacles far and free—
Up domes—up spires—up kingly halls—
Up fanes—up Babylon-like walls—
Up shadowy long-forgotten bowers
Of sculptured ivy and stone flowers—
Up many and many a marvellous shrine
Whose wreathèd friezes intertwine
The viol, the violet, and the vine.

Resignedly beneath the sky
The melancholy waters lie.
So blend the turrets and shadows there
That all seem pendulous in air,
While from a proud tower in the town
Death looks gigantically down.

There open fanes and gaping graves
Yawn level with the luminous waves;
But not the riches there that lie
In each idol's diamond eye—
Not the gaily-jewelled dead
Tempt the waters from their bed;
For no ripples curl, alas!
Along that wilderness of glass—
No swellings tell that winds may be
Upon some far-off happier sea—
No heavings hint that winds have been
On seas less hideously serene.

But lo, a stir is in the air!
The wave—there is a movement there!
As if the towers had thrust aside,
In slightly sinking, the dull tide—
As if their tops had feebly given
A void within the filmy Heaven.
The waves have now a redder glow—
The hours are breathing faint and low—
And when, amid no earthly moans,
Down, down that town shall settle hence,
Hell, rising from a thousand thrones,
Shall do it reverence.

The Sleeper

At midnight, in the month of June,
I stand beneath the mystic moon.
An opiate vapour, dewy, dim,
Exhales from out her golden rim,
And, softly dripping, drop by drop,
Upon the quiet mountain top,
Steals drowsily and musically
Into the universal valley.
The rosemary nods upon the grave;
The lily lolls upon the wave;
Wrapping the fog about its breast,
The ruin moulders into rest;
Looking like Lethe, see! the lake
A conscious slumber seems to take,
And would not, for the world, awake.
All Beauty sleeps!—and lo! where lies
Irene, with her Destinies!

Oh, lady bright! can it be right—
This window open to the night?
The wanton airs, from the tree-top,
Laughingly through the lattice drop—
The bodiless airs, a wizard rout,
Flit through thy chamber in and out,
And wave the curtain canopy
So fitfully—so fearfully—
Above the closed and fringèd lid
'Neath which thy slumb'ring soul lies hid,
That, o'er the floor and down the wall,
Like ghosts the shadows rise and fall!
Oh, lady dear, hast thou no fear?
Why and what art thou dreaming here?
Sure thou art come o'er far-off seas,

A wonder to these garden trees!
Strange is thy pallor! strange thy dress!
Strange, above all, thy length of tress,
And this all solemn silentness!

The lady sleeps! Oh, may her sleep,
Which is enduring, so be deep!
Heaven have her in its sacred keep!
This chamber changed for one more holy,
This bed for one more melancholy,
I pray to God that she may lie
Forever with unopened eye,
While the pale sheeted ghosts go by!

My love, she sleeps! Oh, may her sleep,
As it is lasting, so be deep!
Soft may the worms about her creep!
Far in the forest, dim and old,
For her may some tall vault unfold—
Some vault that oft hath flung its black
And wingèd panels fluttering back,
Triumphant, o'er the crested palls
Of her grand family funerals—

Some sepulchre, remote, alone,
Against whose portal she hath thrown,
In childhood, many an idle stone—
Some tomb from out whose sounding door
She ne'er shall force an echo more,
Thrilling to think, poor child of sin!
It was the dead who groaned within.

Lenore

Ah, broken is the golden bowl!—the spirit flown
   forever!
Let the bell toll!—a saintly soul floats on the Stygian
   river:—
And, Guy de Vere, hast *thou* no tear?—weep now or
   never more!
See! on yon drear and rigid bier low lies thy love,
   Lenore!
Come, let the burial rite be read—the funeral song be
   sung!—
An anthem for the queenliest dead that ever died so
   young—
A dirge for her the doubly dead in that she died so
   young.

"Wretches! ye loved her for her wealth, and ye hated
   her for her pride;
And, when she fell in feeble health, ye blessed her—
   that she died:—
How *shall* the ritual, then, be read—the requiem how
   be sung
By you—by yours, the evil eye,—by yours, the
   slanderous tongue
That did to death the innocence that died, and died so
   young?"

Peccavimus; yet rave not thus! but let a Sabbath song
Go up to God so solemnly the dead may feel no
   wrong!
The sweet Lenore hath gone before, with Hope that
   flew beside,
Leaving thee wild for the dear child that should have
   been thy bride—

For her, the fair and debonair, that now so lowly lies,
The life upon her yellow hair, but not within her
  eyes—
The life still there upon her hair, the death upon her
  eyes.

"Avaunt!—avaunt! to friends from fiends the indignant
  ghost is riven—
From Hell unto a high estate within the utmost
  Heaven—
From moan and groan to a golden throne beside the
  king of Heaven:—
Let *no* bell toll, then, lest her soul, amid its hallowed
  mirth,
Should catch the note as it doth float up from the
  damnèd Earth!
And I—tonight my heart is light:—no dirge will I
  upraise,
But waft the angel on her flight with a Paean of old
  days!"

The Valley of Unrest

Once it smiled a silent dell
Where the people did not dwell;
They had gone unto the wars,
Trusting to the mild-eyed stars,
Nightly, from their azure towers,
To keep watch above the flowers,
In the midst of which all day
The red sun-light lazily lay.
Now each visitor shall confess
The sad valley's restlessness.
Nothing there is motionless—
Nothing save the airs that brood
Over the magic solitude.
Ah, by no wind are stirred those trees
That palpitate like the chill seas
Around the misty Hebrides!
Ah, by no wind those clouds are driven
That rustle through the unquiet Heaven
Uneasily, from morn till even,
Over the violets there that lie
In myriad types of the human eye—
Over the lilies there that wave
And weep above a nameless grave!
They wave:—from out their fragrant tops
Eternal dews come down in drops.
They weep:—from off their delicate stems
Perennial tears descend in gems.

The Coliseum

Type of the antique Rome! Rich reliquary
Of lofty contemplation left to Time
By buried centuries of pomp and power!
At length—at length—after so many days
Of weary pilgrimage and burning thirst
(Thirst for the springs of lore that in thee lie),
I kneel, an altered and an humble man,
Amid thy shadows, and so drink within
My very soul thy grandeur, gloom, and glory!

Vastness! and Age! and Memories of Eld!
Silence! and Desolation! and dim Night!
I feel ye now—I feel ye in your strength—
O spells more sure than e'er Judaean king
Taught in the gardens of Gethsemane!
O charms more potent than the rapt Chaldee
Ever drew down from out the quiet stars!

Here, where a hero fell, a column falls!
Here, where the mimic eagle glared in gold,
A midnight vigil holds the swarthy bat!
Here, where the dames of Rome their gilded hair
Waved to the wind, now wave the reed and thistle!
Here, where on golden throne the monarch lolled,
Glides, spectre-like, unto his marble home,
Lit by the wan light of the hornèd moon,
The swift and silent lizard of the stones!

But stay! these walls—these ivy-clad arcades—
These mouldering plinths—these sad and blackened
    shafts—
These vague entablatures—this crumbling frieze—
These shattered cornices—this wreck—this ruin—

These stones—alas! these gray stones—are they all—
All of the famed and the colossal left
By the corrosive Hours to Fate and me?

"Not all"—the Echoes answer me—"not all!
Prophetic sounds and loud, arise forever
From us, and from all Ruin, unto the wise,
As melody from Memnon to the Sun.
We rule the hearts of mightiest men—we rule
With a despotic sway all giant minds.
We are not impotent—we pallid stones.
Not all our power is gone—not all our fame—
Not all the magic of our high renown—
Not all the wonder that encircles us—
Not all the mysteries that in us lie—
Not all the memories that hang upon
And cling around about us as a garment,
Clothing us in a robe of more than glory."

To One in Paradise

Thou wast that all to me, love,
    For which my soul did pine—
A green isle in the sea, love,
    A fountain and a shrine,
All wreathed with fairy fruits and flowers,
    And all the flowers were mine.
Ah, dream too bright to last!
    Ah, starry Hope! that didst arise
But to be overcast!
    A voice from out the Future cries,
"On! on!"—but o'er the Past
    (Dim gulf!) my spirit hovering lies
Mute, motionless, aghast!

For, alas! alas! with me
    The light of Life is o'er!
No more—no more—no more—
    (Such language holds the solemn sea
To the sands upon the shore)
    Shall bloom the thunder-blasted tree,
Or the stricken eagle soar!

And all my days are trances,
    And all my nightly dreams
Are where thy grey eye glances,
    And where thy footstep gleams—
In what ethereal dances,
    By what eternal streams.

Hymn

At morn—at noon—at twilight dim—
Maria! thou hast heard my hymn!
In joy and wo—in good and ill—
Mother of God, be with me still!
When the Hours flew brightly by,
And not a cloud obscured the sky,
My soul, lest it should truant be,
Thy grace did guide to thine and thee;
Now, when storms of Fate o'ercast
Darkly my Present and my Past,
Let my Future radiant shine
With sweet hopes of thee and thine!

To F—

Beloved! amid the earnest woes
   That crowd around my earthly path—
(Drear path, alas! where grows
Not even one lonely rose)—
   My soul at least a solace hath
In dreams of thee, and therein knows
An Eden of bland repose.

And thus thy memory is to me
   Like some enchanted far-off isle
In some tumultuous sea—
Some ocean throbbing far and free
   With storms—but where meanwhile
Serenest skies continually
Just o'er that one bright island smile.

To F——s S. O——d

Thou wouldst be loved?—then let thy heart
    From its present pathway part not!
Being everything which now thou art,
    Be nothing which thou art not.
So with the world thy gentle ways,
    Thy grace, thy more than beauty,
Shall be an endless theme of praise,
And love—a simple duty.

Bridal Ballad

The ring is on my hand,
   And the wreath is on my brow;
Satins and jewels grand
Are all at my command,
   And I am happy now.

And my lord he loves me well;
   But, when first he breathed his vow,
I felt my bosom swell—
For the words rang as a knell,
And the voice seemed *his* who fell
In the battle down the dell,
   And who is happy now.

But he spoke to re-assure me,
   And he kissed my pallid brow,
While a reverie came o'er me,
And to the church-yard bore me,
And I sighed to him before me
(Thinking him dead D'Elormie),
   "Oh, I am happy now!"

And thus the words were spoken,
   And this the plighted vow;
And, though my faith be broken,
And, though my heart be broken,
Here is a ring as token
   That I am happy now!—
Behold the golden token
   That *proves* me happy now!

Would God I could awaken!
   For I dream I know not how,

And my soul is sorely shaken
Lest an evil step be taken,—
Lest the dead who is forsaken
  May not be happy now.

Sonnet—To Zante

Fair isle, that from the fairest of all flowers
   Thy gentlest of all gentle names dost take,
   How many thoughts of what entombèd hopes!
   At sight of thee and thine at once awake!
How many scenes of what departed bliss!
   How many thoughts of what entombèd hopes!
How many visions of a maiden that is
   No more—no more upon thy verdant slopes!
No more! alas, that magical sad sound
   Transforming all! Thy charms shall please *no more,*—
Thy memory *no more*! Accursèd ground
   Henceforth I hold thy flower-enamelled shore,
O hyacinthine isle! O purple Zante!
"Isola d'oro! Fior di Levante!"

The Haunted Palace

In the greenest of our valleys,
  By good angels tenanted,
Once a fair and stately palace—
  Radiant palace—reared its head.
In the monarch Thought's dominion—
  It stood there!
Never seraph spread a pinion
  Over fabric half so fair!

Banners yellow, glorious, golden,
  On its roof did float and flow,
(This—all this—was in the olden
  Time long ago,)
And every gentle air that dallied,
  In that sweet day,
Along the ramparts plumed and pallid,
  A wingèd odor went away.

Wanderers in that happy valley,
  Through two luminous windows, saw
Spirits moving musically
  To a lute's well-tunèd law,
Round about a throne, where sitting,
  Porphyrogene!
In state his glory well befitting,
  The ruler of the realm was seen.

And all with pearl and ruby glowing
  Was the fair palace door,
Through which came flowing, flowing, flowing,
  And sparkling evermore,
A troop of Echoes, whose sweet duty
  Was but to sing,

In voices of surpassing beauty,
  The wit and wisdom of their king.

But evil things, in robes of sorrow,
  Assailed the monarch's high estate.
(Ah, let us mourn!—for never morrow
  Shall dawn upon him, desolate!)
And round about his home the glory
  That blushed and bloomed,
Is but a dim-remembered story
  Of the old time entombed.

And travellers, now, within that valley,
  Through the red-litten windows see
Vast forms that move fantastically
  To a discordant melody,
While, like a ghastly rapid river,
  Through the pale door
A hideous throng rush out forever,
  And laugh—but smile no more.

Sonnet—Silence

There are some qualities—some incorporate things,
  That have a double life, which thus is made
A type of that twin entity which springs
  From matter and light, evinced in solid and shade.
There is a two-fold *Silence*—sea and shore—
  Body and soul. One dwells in lonely places,
  Newly with grass o'ergrown; some solemn graces,
Some human memories and tearful lore,
Render him terrorless: his name's "No More."
He is the corporate Silence: dread him not!
  No power hath he of evil in himself;
But should some urgent fate (untimely lot!)
  Bring thee to meet his shadow (nameless elf,
That haunteth the lone regions where hath trod
No foot of man,) commend thyself to God!

The Conqueror Worm

Lo! 't is a gala night
  Within the lonesome latter years!
An angel throng, bewinged, bedight
  In veils, and drowned in tears,
Sit in a theatre, to see
  A play of hopes and fears,
While the orchestra breathes fitfully
  The music of the spheres.

Mimes, in the form of God on high,
  Mutter and mumble low,
And hither and thither fly—
  Mere puppets they, who come and go
At bidding of vast formless things
  That shift the scenery to and fro,
Flapping from out their Condor wings
  Invisible Wo!

That motley drama—oh, be sure
  It shall not be forgot!
With its Phantom chased for evermore
  By a crowd that seize it not,
Through a circle that ever returneth in
  To the self-same spot,
And much of Madness, and more of Sin,
  And Horror the soul of the plot.

But see, amid the mimic rout,
  A crawling shape intrude!
A blood-red thing that writhes from out
  The scenic solitude!
It writhes!—it writhes!—with mortal pangs
  The mimes become its food,

And seraphs sob at vermin fangs
  In human gore imbued.

Out—out are the lights—out all!
  And, over each quivering form,
The curtain, a funeral pall,
  Comes down with the rush of a storm,
While the angels, all pallid and wan,
  Uprising, unveiling, affirm
That the play is the tragedy, "Man,"
  And its hero, the Conqueror Worm.

Dream-Land

By a route obscure and lonely,
Haunted by ill angels only,
Where an Eidolon, named NIGHT,
On a black throne reigns upright,
I have reached these lands but newly
From an ultimate dim Thule—
From a wild weird clime that lieth, sublime,
     Out of SPACE—out of TIME.

Bottomless vales and boundless floods,
And chasms, and caves, and Titan woods,
With forms that no man can discover
For the tears that drip all over;
Mountains toppling evermore
Into seas without a shore;
Seas that restlessly aspire,
Surging, unto skies of fire;
Lakes that endlessly outspread
Their lone waters—lone and dead,—
Their still waters—still and chilly
With the snows of the lolling lily.

By the lakes that thus outspread
Their lone waters, lone and dead,—
Their sad waters, sad and chilly
With the snows of the lolling lily—
By the mountains—near the river
Murmuring lowly, murmuring ever,—
By the grey woods,—by the swamp
Where the toad and the newt encamp,—
By the dismal tarns and pools
     Where dwell the Ghouls,—
By each spot the most unholy—

In each nook most melancholy,—
There the traveller meets, aghast,
Sheeted Memories of the Past—
Shrouded forms that start and sigh
As they pass the wanderer by—
White-robed forms of friends long given,
In agony, to the Earth—and Heaven.

For the heart whose woes are legion
'T is a peaceful, soothing region—
For the spirit that walks in shadow
'T is—oh, 't is an Eldorado!
But the traveller, travelling through it,
May not—dare not openly view it;
Never its mysteries are exposed
To the weak human eye unclosed;
So wills its King, who hath forbid
The uplifting of the fringèd lid;
And thus the sad Soul that here passes
Beholds it but through darkened glasses.

By a route obscure and lonely,
Haunted by ill angels only,
Where an Eidolon, named NIGHT,
On a black throne reigns upright,
I have wandered home but newly
From this ultimate dim Thule.

The Raven

Once upon a midnight dreary, while I pondered,
  weak and weary,
Over many a quaint and curious volume of
  forgotten lore—
While I nodded, nearly napping, suddenly there
  came a tapping,
As of some one gently rapping, rapping at my
  chamber door.
" 'Tis some visitor," I muttered, "tapping at my
  chamber door—
              Only this and nothing more."

Ah, distinctly I remember it was in the bleak
  December;
And each separate dying ember wrought its ghost
  upon the floor.
Eagerly I wished the morrow;—vainly I had
  sought to borrow
From my books surcease of sorrow—sorrow
  for the lost Lenore—
For the rare and radiant maiden whom the angels
  name Lenore—
              Nameless *here* for evermore.

And the silken, sad, uncertain rustling of each
  purple curtain
Thrilled me—filled me with fantastic terrors
  never felt before;
So that now, to still the beating of my heart,
  I stood repeating,

" 'Tis some visitor entreating entrance at my
  chamber door—
Some late visitor entreating entrance at my
  chamber door;—
                    This it is and nothing more."

Presently my soul grew stronger; hesitating
  then no longer,
"Sir," said I, "or Madam, truly your forgiveness
  I implore;
But the fact is I was napping, and so gently you
  came rapping,
And so faintly you came tapping, tapping at my
  chamber door,
That I scarce was sure I heard you"—here I
  opened wide the door;—
                    Darkness there and nothing more.

Deep into that darkness peering, long I stood
  there wondering, fearing,
Doubting, dreaming dreams no mortal ever
  dared to dream before;
But the silence was unbroken, and the stillness
  gave no token,
And the only word there spoken was the whispered
  word, "Lenore?"
This I whispered, and an echo murmured back
  the word "Lenore!"
                    Merely this and nothing more.

Back into the chamber turning, all my soul within
    me burning,
Soon again I heard a tapping somewhat louder
    than before.
"Surely," said I, "surely that is something at my
    window lattice;
Let me see, then, what thereat is, and this mystery
    explore—
Let my heart be still a moment and this mystery
    explore;—
            'Tis the wind and nothing more!"

Open here I flung the shutter, when, with many
    a flirt and flutter,
In there stepped a stately Raven of the saintly
    days of yore;
Not the least obeisance made he; not a minute
    stopped or stayed he;
But, with mien of lord or lady, perched above
    my chamber door—
Perched upon a bust of Pallas just above my
    chamber door—
            Perched, and sat, and nothing more.

Then this ebony bird beguiling my sad fancy
    into smiling,
By the grave and stern decorum of the countenance
    it wore,
"Though thy crest be shorn and shaven, thou,"
    I said, "art sure no craven,
Ghastly grim and ancient Raven wandering from
    the Nightly shore—
Tell me what thy lordly name is on the Night's
    Plutonian shore!"
            Quoth the raven, "Nevermore."

Much I marvelled this ungainly fowl to hear
  discourse so plainly,
Though its answer little meaning—little relevancy
  bore;
For we cannot help agreeing that no living
  human being
Ever yet was blessed with seeing bird above
  his chamber door—
Bird or beast upon the sculptured bust above his
  chamber door,
          With such name as "Nevermore."

But the Raven, sitting lonely on the placid bust,
  spoke only
That one word, as if his soul in that one word
  he did outpour.
Nothing farther then he uttered—not a feather
  then he fluttered—
Till I scarcely more than muttered, "Other friends
  have flown before—
On the morrow *he* will leave me, as my Hopes
  have flown before."
          Then the bird said, "Nevermore."

Startled at the stillness broken by reply so aptly
  spoken,
"Doubtless," said I, "what it utters is its only
  stock and store
Caught from some unhappy master whom
  unmerciful Disaster
Followed fast and followed faster till his songs
  one burden bore—
Till the dirges of his Hope that melancholy
  burden bore
          Of 'Never—nevermore.' "

But the Raven still beguiling all my fancy into smiling,
Straight I wheeled a cushioned seat in front of bird,
   and bust and door;
Then, upon the velvet sinking, I betook myself
   to linking
Fancy unto fancy, thinking what this ominous
   bird of yore—
What this grim, ungainly, ghastly, gaunt, and
   ominous bird of yore
             Meant in croaking "Nevermore."

This I sat engaged in guessing, but no syllable
   expressing
To the fowl whose fiery eyes now burned into
   my bosom's core;
This and more I sat divining, with my head at
   ease reclining
On the cushion's velvet lining that the lamp-light
   gloated o'er,
But whose velvet-violet lining with the lamp-light
   gloating o'er,
             She shall press, ah, nevermore!

Then, methought, the air grew denser, perfumed
   from an unseen censer
Swung by Seraphim whose foot-falls tinkled on
   the tufted floor.
"Wretch," I cried, "thy God hath lent thee—by
   these angels he hath sent thee
Respite—respite and nepenthe from thy memories
   of Lenore;
Quaff, oh, quaff this kind nepenthe and forget
   this lost Lenore!"
             Quoth the Raven, "Nevermore."

"Prophet!" said I, "thing of evil!—prophet still,
   if bird or devil!—
Whether Tempter sent, or whether tempest tossed
   thee here ashore,
Desolate yet all undaunted, on this desert land
   enchanted—
On this home by Horror haunted—tell me truly,
   I implore—
Is there—*is* there balm in Gilead?—tell me—tell me,
   I implore!"
         Quoth the Raven, "Nevermore."

"Prophet!" said I, "thing of evil!—prophet still,
   if bird or devil!
By that Heaven that bends above us—by that God
   we both adore—
Tell this soul with sorrow laden if, within the
   distant Aidenn,
It shall clasp a sainted maiden whom the angels
   name Lenore—
Clasp a rare and radiant maiden whom the angels
   name Lenore."
         Quoth the Raven, "Nevermore."

"Be that word our sign of parting, bird or fiend!"
   I shrieked, upstarting—
"Get thee back into the tempest and the Night's
   Plutonian shore!
Leave no black plume as a token of that lie thy
   soul hath spoken!
Leave my loneliness unbroken!—quit the bust
   above my door!
Take thy beak from out my heart, and take thy
   form from off my door!"
         Quoth the Raven, "Nevermore."

And the Raven, never flitting, still is sitting,
   still is sitting
On the pallid bust of Pallas just above my
   chamber door;
And his eyes have all the seeming of a demon's
   that is dreaming,
And the lamp-light o'er him streaming throws
   his shadow on the floor;
And my soul from out that shadow that lies floating
   on the floor

              Shall be lifted—nevermore!

Eulalie—A Song

I dwelt alone
In a world of moan,
And my soul was a stagnant tide,
Till the fair and gentle Eulalie became my blushing
bride—
Till the yellow-haired young Eulalie became my
smiling bride.

Ah, less—less bright
The stars of the night
Than the eyes of the radiant girl!
And never a flake
That the vapor can make
With the moon-tints of purple and pearl,
Can vie with the modest Eulalie's most unregarded
curl—
Can compare with the bright-eyed Eulalie's most
humble and careless curl.

Now Doubt—now Pain
Come never again,
For her soul gives me sigh for sigh,
And all day long
Shines, bright and strong,
Astarte within the sky,
While ever to her dear Eulalie upturns her matron
eye—
While ever to her young Eulalie upturns her violet eye.

A Valentine

For her these lines are penned, whose luminous eyes,
   Brightly expressive as the twins of Loeda,
Shall find her own sweet name that, nestling, lies
   Upon this page, enwrapped from every reader.
Search narrowly this rhyme, which holds a treasure
   Divine—a talisman—an amulet
That must be worn at heart. Search well the measure;
   The words—the letters themselves. Do not forget
The trivialest point, or you may lose your labor.
   And yet there is in this no Gordian knot
Which one might not undo without a sabre,
   If one could merely understand the plot.
Enwritten upon this page whereon are peering
   Such eager eyes, there lies, I say, *perdu,*
A well-known name, oft uttered in the hearing
   Of poets, by poets; as the name is a poet's, too.
Its letters, although naturally lying—
   Like the knight Pinto (Mendez Ferdinando)—
Still form a synonym for truth. Cease trying!
   You will not read the riddle though you do the best
   you *can* do.

To M. L. S——

Of all who hail thy presence as the morning—
Of all to whom thine absence is the night—
The blotting utterly from out high heaven
The sacred sun—of all who, weeping, bless thee
Hourly for hope—for life—ah! above all,
For the resurrection of deep-buried faith
In Truth, in Virtue, in Humanity—
Of all who, on Despair's unhallowed bed
Lying down to die, have suddenly arisen
At thy soft-murmured words, "Let there be light!"
At the soft-murmured words that were fulfilled
In the seraphic glancing of thine eyes—
Of all who owe thee most—whose gratitude
Nearest resembles worship—oh, remember
The truest—the most fervently devoted,
And think that these weak lines are written by him—
By him who, as he pens them, thrills to think
His spirit is communing with an angel's.

Ulalume — A Ballad

The skies they were ashen and sober;
    The leaves they were crispèd and sere—
    The leaves they were withering and sere:
It was night, in the lonesome October
    Of my most immemorial year:
It was hard by the dim lake of Auber,
    In the misty mid region of Weir—
It was down by the dank tarn of Auber,
    In the ghoul-haunted woodland of Weir.

Here once, through an alley Titanic,
    Of cypress, I roamed with my Soul—
    Of cypress, with Psyche, my Soul.
These were days when my heart was volcanic
    As the scoriac rivers that roll—
    As the lavas that restlessly roll
Their sulphurous currents down Yaanek
    In the ultimate climes of the Pole—
That groan as they roll down Mount Yaanek
    In the realms of the Boreal Pole.

Our talk had been serious and sober,
    But our thoughts they were palsied and
  sere—
    Our memories were treacherous and sere—
For we knew not the month was October,
    And we marked not the night of the year
    (Ah, night of all nights in the year!)—
We noted not the dim lake of Auber
    (Though once we had journeyed down
  here)—
We remembered not the dank tarn of Auber,
    Nor the ghoul-haunted woodland of Weir.

And now, as the night was senescent
    And star-dials pointed to morn—
    As the star-dials hinted of morn—
At the end of our path a liquescent
    And nebulous lustre was born,
Out of which a miraculous crescent
    Arose with a duplicate horn—
Astarte's bediamonded crescent
    Distinct with its duplicate horn.

And I said: "She is warmer than Dian;
    She rolls through an ether of sighs—
    She revels in a region of sighs.
She has seen that the tears are not dry on
    These cheeks, where the worm never dies,
And has come past the stars of the Lion,
    To point us the path to the skies—
    To the Lethean peace of the skies—
Come up, in despite of the Lion,
    To shine on us with her bright eyes—
Come up through the lair of the Lion,
    With love in her luminous eyes."

But Psyche, uplifting her finger,
    Said: "Sadly this star I mistrust—
    Her pallor I strangely mistrust:
Ah, hasten!—ah, let us not linger!
    Ah, fly!—let us fly!—for we must."
In terror she spoke, letting sink her
    Wings until they trailed in the dust—
In agony sobbed, letting sink her
    Plumes till they trailed in the dust—
    Till they sorrowfully trailed in the dust.

I replied: "This is nothing but dreaming:
    Let us on by this tremulous light!
    Let us bathe in this crystalline light!
Its Sibyllic splendor is beaming
    With Hope and in Beauty to-night:—
    See!—it flickers up the sky through the night!
Ah, we safely may trust to its gleaming,
    And be sure it will lead us aright—
We surely may trust to a gleaming
    That cannot but guide us aright,
    Since it flickers up to Heaven through the
  night."

Thus I pacified Psyche and kissed her,
    And tempted her out of her gloom—
    And conquered her scruples and gloom;
And we passed to the end of the vista,
    But were stopped by the door of a tomb—
    By the door of a legended tomb;
And I said—"What is written, sweet sister,
    On the door of this legended tomb?"
    She replied: "Ulalume—Ulalume!—
    'Tis the vault of thy lost Ulalume!"

Then my heart it grew ashen and sober
    As the leaves that were crispèd and sere—
    As the leaves that were withering and sere;
And I cried: "It was surely October
    On *this* very night of last year
    That I journeyed—I journeyed down here!—
    That I brought a dread burden down here—
    On this night of all nights in the year,
    Ah, what demon has tempted me here?
Well I know, now, this dim lake of Auber—
    This misty mid region of Weir—

Well I know, now, this dank tarn of Auber,
    This ghoul-haunted woodland of Weir."

Said we, then,—the two, then: "Ah, can it
    Have been that the woodlandish ghouls—
    The pitiful, the merciful ghouls—
To bar up our way and to ban it
    From the secret that lies in these wolds—
    From the thing that lies hidden in these wolds—
Have drawn up the spectre of a planet
    From the limbo of lunary souls—
This sinfully scintillant planet
    From the Hell of the planetary souls?"

An Enigma

"Seldom we find," says Solomon Don Dunce,
  "Half an idea in the profoundest sonnet.
Through all the flimsy things we see at once
  As easily as through a Naples bonnet—
  Trash of all trash!—how *can* a lady don it?
Yet heavier far than your Petrarchan stuff—
Owl-downy nonsense that the faintest puff
  Twirls into trunk-paper the while you con it."
And, veritably, Sol is right enough.
The general tuckermanities are arrant
Bubbles—ephemeral and *so* transparent—
But *this* is, now,—you may depend upon it—
Stable, opaque, immortal—all by dint
Of the dear names that lie concealed within 't.

To — — —

Not long ago, the writer of these lines,
In the mad pride of intellectuality,
Maintained "the power of words"—denied that ever
A thought arose within the human brain
Beyond the utterance of the human tongue;
And now, as if in mockery of that boast,
Two words—two foreign soft dissyllables—
Italian tones made only to be murmured
By angels dreaming in the moonlit "dew
That hangs like chains of pearl on Hermon hill"—
Have stirred from out the abysses of his heart,
Unthought-like thoughts that are the souls of thought,
Richer, far wilder, far diviner visions
Than even the seraph harper, Israfel,
Who has "the sweetest voice of all God's creatures,"
Could hope to utter. And I! my spells are broken.
The pen falls powerless from my shivering hand.
With thy dear name as text, though bidden by thee,
I cannot write—I cannot speak or think,
Alas, I cannot feel; for 't is not feeling,
This standing motionless upon the golden
Threshold of the wide-open gate of dreams,
Gazing, entranced, adown the gorgeous vista,
And thrilling as I see upon the right,
Upon the left, and all the way along
Amid empurpled vapors, far away
To where the prospect terminates—*thee only*.

To Helen

I saw thee once—once only—years ago:
I must not say *how* many—but *not* many.
It was a July midnight; and from out
A full-orbed moon, that, like thine own soul, soaring,
Sought a precipitate pathway up through heaven,
There fell a silvery-silken veil of light,
With quietude, and sultriness, and slumber,
Upon the upturn'd faces of a thousand
Roses that grew in an enchanted garden,
Where no wind dared to stir, unless on tiptoe—
Fell on the upturn'd faces of these roses
That gave out, in return for the love-light,
Their odorous souls in an ecstatic death—
Fell on the upturn'd faces of these roses
That smiled and died in this parterre, enchanted
By thee, and by the poetry of thy presence.

Clad all in white, upon a violet bank
I saw thee half reclining; while the moon
Fell on the upturn'd faces of the roses,
And on thine own, upturn'd—alas, in sorrow!

Was it not Fate that, on this July midnight—
Was it not Fate (whose name is also Sorrow)
That bade me pause before that garden-gate,
To breathe the incense of those slumbering roses?
No footstep stirred: the hated world all slept,
Save only thee and me. (Oh, Heaven!—oh, God!
How my heart beats in coupling those two words!
Save only thee and me.) I paused—I looked—
And in an instant all things disappeared.
(Ah, bear in mind this garden was enchanted!)
The pearly lustre of the moon went out:

The mossy banks and the meandering paths,
The happy flowers and the repining trees,
Were seen no more: the very roses' odors
Died in the arms of the adoring airs.
All—all expired save thee—save less than thou:
Save only the divine light in thine eyes—
Save but the soul in thine uplifted eyes.
I saw but them—they were the world to me.
I saw but them—saw only them for hours—
Saw only them until the moon went down.
What wild heart-histories seemed to lie enwritten
Upon those crystalline, celestial spheres!
How dark a wo! yet how sublime a hope!
How silently serene a sea of pride!
How daring an ambition! yet how deep—
How fathomless a capacity for love!

But now, at length, dear Dian sank from sight,
Into a western couch of thunder-cloud;
And thou, a ghost, amid the entombing trees
Didst glide away. *Only thine eyes remained.*
They *would not* go—they never yet have gone.
Lighting my lonely pathway home that night,
They have not left me (as my hopes have) since.
They follow me—they lead me through the years.
They are my ministers—yet I their slave.
Their office is to illumine and enkindle—
My duty, *to be saved* by their bright light,
And purified in their electric fire,
And sanctified in their elysian fire.
They fill my soul with Beauty (which is Hope),
And are far up in Heaven—the stars I kneel to
In the sad, silent watches of my night;
While even in the meridian glare of day
I see them still—two sweetly scintillant
Venuses, unextinguished by the sun!

Eldorado

Gaily bedight,
A gallant knight,
In sunshine and in shadow,
Had journeyed long,
Singing a song,
In search of Eldorado.

But he grew old—
This knight so bold—
And o'er his heart a shadow
Fell as he found
No spot of ground
That looked like Eldorado.

And, as his strength
Failed him at length,
He met a pilgrim shadow—
"Shadow," said he,
"Where can it be—
This land of Eldorado?"

"Over the Mountains
Of the Moon,
Down the Valley of the Shadow,
Ride, boldly ride,"
The shade replied,—
"If you seek for Eldorado!"

For Annie

Thank Heaven! the crisis,
    The danger, is past,
And the lingering illness
    Is over at last—
And the fever called "Living"
    Is conquered at last.

Sadly, I know
    I am shorn of my strength,
And no muscle I move
    As I lie at full length—
But no matter!—I feel
    I am better at length.

And I rest so composedly,
    Now, in my bed,
That any beholder
    Might fancy me dead—
Might start at beholding me,
    Thinking me dead.

The moaning and groaning,
    The sighing and sobbing,
Are quieted now,
    With that horrible throbbing
At heart:—ah, that horrible,
    Horrible throbbing!

The sickness—the nausea—
    The pitiless pain—
Have ceased, with the fever
    That maddened my brain—

With the fever called "Living"
  That burned in my brain.

And oh! of all tortures
  That torture the worst
Has abated—the terrible
  Torture of thirst
For the naphthaline river
  Of Passion accurst:—
I have drank of a water
  That quenches all thirst:—

Of a water that flows,
  With a lullaby sound,
From a spring but a very few
  Feet under ground—
From a cavern not very far
  Down under ground.

And ah! let it never
  Be foolishly said
That my room it is gloomy
  And narrow my bed;
For man never slept
  In a different bed—
And, to *sleep,* you must slumber
  In just such a bed.

My tantalized spirit
  Here blandly reposes,
Forgetting, or never
  Regretting, its roses—
Its old agitations
  Of myrtles and roses:

For now, while so quietly
  Lying, it fancies

A holier odor
    About it, of pansies—
A rosemary odor,
    Commingled with pansies—
With rue and the beautiful
    Puritan pansies.

And so it lies happily,
    Bathing in many
A dream of the truth
    And the beauty of Annie—
Drowned in a bath
    Of the tresses of Annie.

She tenderly kissed me,
    She fondly caressed,
And then I fell gently
    To sleep on her breast—
Deeply to sleep
    From the heaven of her breast.

When the light was extinguished,
    She covered me warm,
And she prayed to the angels
    To keep me from harm—
To the queen of the angels
    To shield me from harm.

And I lie so composedly,
    Now, in my bed,
(Knowing her love),
    That you fancy me dead—
And I rest so contentedly,
    Now, in my bed
(With her love at my breast),
    That you fancy me dead—

That you shudder to look at me,
  Thinking me dead:—

But my heart it is brighter
  Than all of the many
Stars of the sky,
  For it sparkles with Annie—
It glows with the light
  Of the love of my Annie—
With the thought of the light
  Of the eyes of my Annie.

To My Mother

Because I feel that, in the Heavens above,
    The angels, whispering to one another,
Can find, among their burning terms of love,
    None so devotional as that of "Mother,"
Therefore by that dear name I long have called you—
    You who are more than mother unto me,
And fill my heart of hearts, where Death installed you
    In setting my Virginia's spirit free.
My mother—my own mother, who died early,
    Was but the mother of myself; but you
Are mother to the one I loved so dearly,
    And thus are dearer than the mother I knew
By that infinity with which my wife
    Was dearer to my soul than its soul-life.

Annabel Lee

It was many and many a year ago,
　　In a kingdom by the sea,
That a maiden there lived whom you may know
　　By the name of ANNABEL LEE;
And this maiden she lived with no other thought
　　Than to love and be loved by me.

I was a child and *she* was a child,
　　In this kingdom by the sea,
But we loved with a love that was more than love—
　　I and my ANNABEL LEE—
With a love that the wingèd seraphs of Heaven
　　Coveted her and me.

And this was the reason that, long ago,
　　In this kingdom by the sea,
A wind blew out of a cloud, chilling
　　My beautiful ANNABEL LEE;
So that her highborn kinsmen came
　　And bore her away from me,
To shut her up in a sepulchre
　　In this kingdom by the sea.

The angels, not half so happy in Heaven,
　　Went envying her and me:—
Yes!—that was the reason (as all men know,
　　In this kingdom by the sea)
That the wind came out of the cloud by night,
　　Chilling and killing my ANNABEL LEE.

But our love it was stronger by far than the love
　　Of those who were older than we—
　　Of many far wiser than we—

And neither the angels in Heaven above,
    Nor the demons down under the sea,
Can ever dissever my soul from the soul
    Of the beautiful ANNABEL LEE:—

For the moon never beams, without bringing me
  dreams
    Of the beautiful ANNABEL LEE;
And the stars never rise, but I feel the bright eyes
    Of the beautiful ANNABEL LEE:
And so, all the night-tide, I lie down by the side
Of my darling—my darling—my life and my bride,
    In the sepulchre there by the sea—
    In her tomb by the sounding sea.

The Bells

I

Hear the sledges with the bells—
Silver bells!
What a world of merriment their melody foretells!
How they tinkle, tinkle, tinkle,
In the icy air of night!
While the stars that oversprinkle
All the heavens, seem to twinkle
With a crystalline delight;
Keeping time, time, time,
In a sort of Runic rhyme,
To the tintinnabulation that so musically wells
From the bells, bells, bells, bells,
Bells, bells, bells—
From the jingling and the tinkling of the bells.

II

Hear the mellow wedding bells—
Golden bells!
What a world of happiness their harmony foretells!
Through the balmy air of night
How they ring out their delight!—
From the molten-golden notes,
And all in tune,
What a liquid ditty floats
To the turtle-dove that listens, while she gloats
On the moon!
Oh, from out the sounding cells,
What a gush of euphony voluminously wells!
How it swells!
How it dwells

On the Future!—how it tells
Of the rapture that impels
To the swinging and the ringing
Of the bells, bells, bells—
Of the bells, bells, bells, bells,
Bells, bells, bells—
To the rhyming and the chiming of the bells!

III

Hear the loud alarum bells—
Brazen bells!
What a tale of terror, now, their turbulency tells!
In the startled ear of night
How they scream out their affright!
Too much horrified to speak,
They can only shriek, shriek,
Out of tune,
In a clamorous appealing to the mercy of the fire,
In a mad expostulation with the deaf and frantic fire,
Leaping higher, higher, higher,
With a desperate desire,
And a resolute endeavor
Now—now to sit, or never,
By the side of the pale-faced moon.
Oh, the bells, bells, bells!
What a tale their terror tells
Of Despair!
How they clang, and clash, and roar!
What a horror they outpour
On the bosom of the palpitating air!
Yet the ear, it fully knows,
By the twanging
And the clanging,
How the danger ebbs and flows;
Yet the ear distinctly tells,

In the jangling,
And the wrangling,
How the danger sinks and swells,
By the sinking or the swelling in the anger of the bells—
Of the bells—
Of the bells, bells, bells, bells,
Bells, bells, bells—
In the clamor and the clangor of the bells!

IV

Hear the tolling of the bells—
Iron bells!
What a world of solemn thought their monody compels!
In the silence of the night,
How we shiver with affright
At the melancholy menace of their tone!
For every sound that floats
From the rust within their throats
Is a groan.
And the people—ah, the people—
They that dwell up in the steeple,
All alone,
And who, tolling, tolling, tolling,
In that muffled monotone,
Feel a glory in so rolling
On the human heart a stone—
They are neither man nor woman—
They are neither brute nor human—
They are Ghouls:—
And their king it is who tolls:—
And he rolls, rolls, rolls, rolls,
Rolls
A paean from the bells!
And his merry bosom swells
With the paean of the bells!

And he dances, and he yells;
Keeping time, time, time,
In a sort of Runic rhyme,
To the paean of the bells—
Of the bells:
Keeping time, time, time
In a sort of Runic rhyme,
To the throbbing of the bells—
Of the bells, bells, bells—
To the sobbing of the bells:—
Keeping time, time, time,
As he knells, knells, knells,
In a happy Runic rhyme,
To the rolling of the bells—
Of the bells, bells, bells—
To the tolling of the bells—
Of the bells, bells, bells, bells,
Bells, bells, bells—
To the moaning and the groaning of the bells.

AFTERWORD

Returning to the poems of Edgar Allan Poe, I find myself amazed by how many lines and phrases I already know by heart, and this is surely a common experience for readers. "Quoth the raven, 'Nevermore' "; "the pallid bust of Pallas"; " 'Twas many and many a year ago, / In a kingdom by the sea"; "the glory that was Greece and the grandeur that was Rome"—these passages and dozens of others can be found in the great collective warehouse of tags where nursery rhymes, lines from Shakespeare, ballads, scraps from the Bible, and lullabies are also stored. If it seems that Poe's poems are just a little over-the-top, and that to love them as I do may be an embarrassing lapse in taste, the central fact of their tenacity rebukes any easy dismissal—as does the sheer enjoyment many of us experience on reading them, aloud, again and again. "Lenore," "Ulalume," and "The Bells" unfailingly fill the mouth and ears with pleasure; the early poem "Sonnet—To Science" has that unforgettable final line: "The summer dream beneath the tamarind tree"; and even some of the less familiar ones, such as "Bridal Ballad," or the heart-wrenching "Alone," have the miraculous quality of seeming to be known before they are read, so that they are simultaneously mysterious and familiar, like the old friend who suddenly astonishes you with his strangeness or the new acquaintance whom you are convinced you must have known since childhood.

How is it that Poe's words have this power to inhabit our psyches? One answer has to do with the peculiar charms of his prosody, about which more later. But additionally, if we can somehow scrape away the legends and clichés—that famous photograph that makes him look so sinister; the B-horror-movie versions of his tales; our gloomy knowledge of his strange marriage, poverty, and early death—if we can try to see Poe as a writer afresh, we may be struck by some unexpected qualities. First, that he is very funny—even in his serious stories and poems, a sense of buffoonery and self-mockery is never far from the surface. (In his famous essay about the composition of "The Raven," he admits that he "approach[ed] as nearly to the ludicrous as was admissible.") Humor, mixed as it is in Poe's imagination with so many somber and melancholy themes, brings an added flavor, like salt in a sugary treat that makes the whole irresistible. At least as compelling is that in his stories and to a certain extent in his poems, he created a particular American hero—the naïf led astray, often by the dark and sophisticated charms of the Old World.

Take "The Pit and the Pendulum," one of his most famous stories. The narrator finds himself undergoing the tortures of the Spanish Inquisition—and although a trial is alluded to, there is no suggestion as to the nature of the supposed crimes for which he was condemned; and indeed, the innocence of the narrator and the arbitrariness of his fate is a given of the tale. In "The Fall of the House of Usher," an unsuspecting fellow falls into a world of decayed English aristocracy and fetid sexuality. Nearly all the tales are set in the cities and country houses of the Old World: Paris is a city of terror in "The Murders in the Rue Morgue," and Rome's catacombs swallow up the narrator of "The Cask of Amontillado." In the poems, as well, although the locales are rarely given precisely, there is an overwhelming feel of the Old World—in multiple allusions to classical literature, in the evocation of fairy-tale kingdoms, in the German, Norman, and Mediterranean place-names. In his Eurocentricity, Poe's inclinations accorded with those of many others in early-nineteenth-century America. But in the way in which he emphasized the *alien* quality of the Old World, even as he focused his attention upon it—by having a sort of Ordinary Joe, or Ordinary Edgar, seduced and beset by its archaic strangeness—he created a new type that many subsequent writers explored. Think of the "innocent" Twain who went abroad, think of Hawthorne's Italian stories, and think perhaps especially of Henry James's American men and women plunged, in all their ignorant glory, into the mires of European intrigue.

Poe's imaginative use of Europe had some of its origins in his own biography. Born to a pair of traveling actors and deposited at an early age with wealthy Virginia relatives, he was while still a boy taken to England and enrolled in a boarding school. While there is every evidence that he valued his education, his recurrence to the theme of the young man in strange Old World circumstances, reimagined as tales of horror, surely began with the strong impressions made on a lonely boy. In England he was also infused with the lifelong certainty that English tastes and education were superior, as were European architecture, furnishings, art, and literature. The high-handed snobbery that characterized his later criticism, and his disdain for most things American, reveal the gnawing fear of inferiority that such an attitude inevitably engendered.

A profound uneasiness reveals itself, in Poe's essays especially—a sense of his trying too hard. Poe's essay "The Philosophy of Furniture," while certainly amusing in its attack on American middle-class bad taste, can also be painful in its implicit self-disgust. "There could be nothing more directly offensive to the eye of an artist than the interior of what is termed in the United States . . . a well-furnished apartment." He complains of American taste as "preposterous" in its penchant for "straight lines" and "glare," and disapproves of the use of gas for indoor lighting. Poe reaches for classical—especially Greek—models for alternatives. In this, Poe was actually no maverick; most of American high-cultural taste for the first half of the nineteenth century was already exhibiting this predilection, in its columns, Empire couches, parquet floors, and curvy klismos chairs. When, at the conclusion of the sketch, Poe conjures up a perfect room—with "two large low sofas of rose-wood and crimson-silk," "four large and gorgeous Sevres vases, in which bloom a profusion of sweet and vivid flowers," and "a tall candelabrum, bearing a small antique lamp with a highly perfumed oil"—I am struck as much by the enchantments of wealth as with the particulars of style. What a contrast to Poe's adult life of grinding poverty, devoid of such luxuries, his imagination offered.

The urge for things classical was not confined to public buildings or the homes of the very rich, however. All across the country in the early nineteenth century, young ladies were being trained to copy classical art; young men wore togas to deliver Latin orations at school; and the Athenaeums of cities and small towns were regularly visited by traveling exhibits of Greek and Roman sculptures, with plaster fig leaves strategically attached. One area of domestic life that also absorbed classical tendencies was the funereal. "Mourning pictures" of the period typically depict an urn, a weeping willow, and a female figure bent over with sorrow. Often an inscription is written on the urn; one example in the Baltimore Museum of Art reads:

A slight memorial of real merit
Solomon Moulton
Died 26 May 1827
Aged 19
HE
was the writer of several poems
in the Lynn Mirror, signed LILLIE

Thy genius gave the wound that laid thee low
And virtue mourns the loss that bids our sorrows flow

The inscription follows the form of the urn, with the rhymed lines as a kind of table beneath the pedestal. The leaves of the willow branches that droop over the lip of the urn are manifold, and fill every corner of the page.

I am arrested by this mourning drawing, for several reasons. First, the mourned young man was a contemporary of Poe's in place and time—and that he seems to have killed himself adds immeasurably to the pathos of their connection. In his most desperate early years, when he had been cut off financially by his adoptive father and expelled from West Point, Poe himself often threatened suicide. (That this Solomon Moulton was probably the sort of poet for whom Poe would have expressed great scorn seems beside the point.)

It seems to me as well that there is an aesthetic connection between such "primitive" or "folk" drawings and Poe's poems. Not only in their melancholy preoccupation, but in their flatness, their literalness, their effort to fill the page with detail, their yearning after classical symmetry, and their effort at memorialization—these pictures suggest another light in which to see Poe's poetry.

His poems are often just a little too long, just a little too much; the effects are sometimes too self-conscious and overdone; and the effort to capture and memorialize certain emotional events can seem strained. Like the artist drawing the weeping willow, Poe fills every inch of his canvas with leaves.

This is not all bad; these drawings can be deeply moving, and pleasing—but we may conclude that, rather than the sophisticated art forms of Attic vases and heroic couplets to which they allude, they are what we call "primitive." They are like a child's version of Greek art, or poetry. Again, with Poe, the childlike timbre of his poetic voice, its appeal to the child within us—is not necessarily a defect, but we must be aware that it is not always what was intended.

Poe wrote longingly of ease, of calm, of sweet sounds and pure love. Like that exquisitely furnished room in "The Philosophy of Furniture," his poems are filled with curves and perfumed oils, with beauty to look at and taste and hear. One notes, in light of his dislike of straight lines, how there are almost no straight lines in his poems—how he chose to fill his stanzas with lines of irregular length curving down the margins, and how he typically disarranged the regimentation of regular iambic verse with the unexpected presence of anapests, trochees, and dactyls.

Since he wrote expansively about his methods of poetic composition, we can be in little doubt that Poe was consciously aiming for certain effects. Like a magician in off-hours, he enjoyed describing in detail how a poem came to be. Indeed, it may be in his own mechanical efforts at effects that he tried too hard, and opened that rift between intention and result. To return to his essay on "The Raven":

> Having made up my mind to a *refrain*, the division of the poem into stanzas as, of course, a corollary; the *refrain* forming the close to each stanza. That such a close, to have force, must be sonorous and susceptible of protracted emphasis, admitted no doubt: and these considerations inevitably led me to the long *o* as the most sonorous vowel, in connection with the *r* as the most producible consonant. The sound of the *refrain* being thus determined, it became necessary to select a word embodying this sound, and at the same time in keeping with the melancholy which I had predetermined as the tone of the poem. In such a search it would have been absolutely impossible to overlook the word "Nevermore." In fact, it was the very first which presented itself.

Do we necessarily believe that this was exactly how "Nevermore" occurred to him? It doesn't matter. His fiction of mastery in his method of composition is telling, even if it is, in part, a fiction.

On several occasions in his adult life, Poe read his poems aloud in public; the effect on his audiences was memorable, and mesmerizing. Later, "The Raven," "The Bells," and "Annabel Lee" all became staples of that Victorian parlor artistry called "melodeclamation," in which a performer would recite the text while a musical composition—written, like a sound track, to swell behind the voice—was played on the piano. Even in the privacy of one's own room, it is almost impossible to read Poe's poems aloud without swaying, gesticulating, and working oneself into a kind of frenzied embodiment of the verses—such is their suggestive power.

These poems cast a spell; they are magical incantations, as Aldous Huxley and Richard Wilbur, among other critics, have noted. Even if we have decided they are childish, even if we have laughed at some of the effects, we are caught by them nonetheless. Repetitions of vowel sounds, onomatopoeia (his use of "tintinnabulation" is a textbook example), and his uncanny knack for hypnotic effects (such as the long *ee* and *em* sounds in "the summer dream beneath the tamarind tree") do not simply describe feeling; they are meant to, and to a large extent do, *create* that feeling. Sometimes he drums like a shaman, as in "The Bells":

> . . . tolling, tolling, tolling,
>   In that muffled monotone,
> Feel a glory in so rolling
>   On the human heart a stone—
> They are neither man nor woman—
> They are neither brute nor human—
>   They are Ghouls:—
> And their king it is who tolls:—
> And he rolls, rolls, rolls,
>   Rolls
> A paean from the bells!

The ancient business of riddles and spells, in which words have the power to create worlds, and to make or unmake the men who seek those worlds, is central to Poe's poetry. What it does to the reader, the listener, is to reduce him or her to a state of goggle-eyed excitement, to the state of a child.

And the voice of the writer? Perhaps it is wrong to say that *his* is the voice of a child; say, rather, that it is that of an older boy, an adolescent who has been somewhere strange ("a kingdom by the sea," "the realms of the Boreal Pole," "a July midnight," "an ultimate dim Thule") and is telling his tale by firelight. Poe wants to enthrall; you wish to be enthralled; his artistry, though at times a trifle bullying and crude, is absolute. You *will* be swept away by the sounds, you *will* be hypnotized; he has you forever, in "a dream within a dream."

—April Bernard

SELECTED
BIBLIOGRAPHY

Works by Edgar Allan Poe

Tamerlane and Other Poems, 1827 Poems
Al Aaraaf, Tamerlane, and Minor Poems, 1829 Poems
Poems: Second Edition, 1831 Poems
"MS Found in a Bottle," 1835 Story
Politian—A Tragedy, 1835 Play
The Narrative of Arthur Gordon Pym of Nantucket, 1838 Novel
Tales of the Grotesque and Arabesque, 2 vols., 1840 Stories
The Prose Romances, 1843 Stories
Tales, 1845 Stories
The Raven and Other Poems, 1845 Poems
Eureka: An Essay on the Material and Spiritual Universe, 1848 Criticism

Anthologies

Harrison, James A., ed. *The Complete Works of Edgar Allan Poe*. 1902. New York: AMS, 1979.
Mabbott, Thomas Ollive, et al., eds. *Collected Works of Edgar Allan Poe*. 3 vols. Cambridge, MA: Harvard University Press, 1969–78.

Pollin, Burton. *The Imaginary Voyages*. Boston: Twayne, 1981.

Stovall, Floyd, ed. *The Poems of Edgar Allan Poe*. Charlottesville: University of Virginia Press, 1965.

Levine, Stuart, and Susan Levine, eds. *The Short Fiction of Edgar Allan Poe: An Annotated Edition*. 2nd ed. Urbana: University of Illinois Press, 1990.

Sisson, C. H., ed. *Edgar Allan Poe: Poems and Essays on Poetry*. London: Carcanet Press, 2006.

SELECTED BIOGRAPHY AND CRITICISM

Alexander, Jean. *Affidavits of Genius: Edgar Allan Poe and the French Critics, 1847–1924*. Port Washington, NY: Kenikat, 1971.

Bloom, Harold. *Edgar Allan Poe*. New York: Facts on File, 2007.

Budd, Lewis J., and Edwin H. Cady, eds. *On Poe: The Best from American Literature*. Durham, NC: Duke University Press, 1993.

Carlson, Eric, ed. *Critical Essays on Edgar Allan Poe*. Boston: G. K. Hall, 1987.

Clark, Graham, ed. *Edgar Allan Poe: Critical Assessments*. 4 vols. East Sussex: Helm Information, 1991.

Fisher, Benjamin Franklin, IV. *Poe and His Times: The Artist and His Milieu*. Baltimore: Edgar Allan Poe Society, 1990.

Hartman, Jonathan. *The Marketing of Edgar Allan Poe*. New York: Routledge, 2008.

Hoffman, Daniel. *Poe, Poe, Poe, Poe, Poe, Poe, Poe*. New York: Doubleday, 1972.

Hyneman, Esther F. *Edgar Allan Poe: An Annotated Bibliography of Books and Articles in English, 1827–1973*. Boston: G. K. Hall, 1974.

Kennedy, J. Gerald. *Poe, Death, and the Life of Writing*. New Haven, CT: Yale University Press, 1987.

Meyers, Jeffrey. "Edgar Allan Poe." *The Columbia History of American Poetry*. Jay Parini, ed. New York: Columbia University Press, 1993.

———. *Edgar Allan Poe: His Life and Legacy*. New York: Scribners, 1992.

Miller, John Carl. *Building Poe Biography*. Baton Rouge: Louisiana State University Press, 1977.

Ostrom, John W., ed. *The Letters of Edgar Allan Poe*. 2 vols. New York: Gordian, 1966.

Peeples, Scott. *The Afterlife of Edgar Allan Poe*. New York: Camden House, 2007.

Poe Studies: Dark Romanticism. Pullman: Washington State University Press (periodical that publishes current Poe bibliography and criticism).

Quinn, Arthur Hobson. *Edgar Allan Poe: A Critical Biography*. Baltimore: Johns Hopkins University Press, 1997.

Reynolds, David S. *Beneath the American Renaissance: The Subversive Imagination in the Age of Emerson and Melville*. Cambridge, MA: Harvard University Press, 1988.

Rosenheim, Shawn, and Stephen Rachman, eds. *The American Face of Edgar Allan Poe*. Baltimore: Johns Hopkins University Press, 1995.

Silverman, Kenneth. *Edgar Allan Poe: Mournful and Never-ending Remembrance*. New York: Harper-Collins, 1991.

Thomas, Dwight, and David K. Jackson. *The Poe Log: A Documentary Life of Edgar Allan Poe 1809–1849*. Boston: G. K. Hall, 1987.

Thompson, G. R., ed. *Edgar Allan Poe: Essays and Revisions*. New York: Library of America, 1984.

Walker, I. M., ed. *Edgar Allan Poe: The Critical Heritage*. London: Routledge and Kegan Paul, 1986.

America's Poetry from Signet Classics

SPOON RIVER ANTHOLOGY by Edgar Lee Masters
A notorious success when first published in 1915, Masters'
collection of free verse monologues is populated by 200 former
inhabitants of an imagined Midwestern town, speaking their
epitaphs from beyond the grave. This is a triumphant
proclamation of the American Spirit, at once moving, literate, and
down home.

POEMS BY ROBERT FROST: A Boy's Will & North of Boston
Frost's first two collections of poetry, published here in their
original form without the revisions and editing that took place in
later years.

THE WASTE LAND & Other Poems by T.S. Eliot
This selection, made by the preeminent critic Helen Vendler,
contains Eliot's most important early work. Here in one volume is
the poetry that so profoundly changed American writing at the
beginning of the 20th century.

Available wherever books are sold or at
penguinrandomhouse.com

READ THE TOP 20
SIGNET CLASSICS

PENGUINRANDOMHOUSE.COM
FACEBOOK.COM/SIGNETCLASSIC

S0154